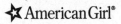

Like Sisters

Caitlin in Charge

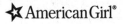
American Girl®

Like Sisters

Caitlin in Charge

by Clare Hutton

Scholastic Press

Published by Scholastic Inc., *Publishers since 1920*. SCHOLASTIC and associated logos are trademarks and/or registered trademarks of Scholastic Inc. The publisher does not have any control over and does not assume any responsibility for author or third-party websites or their content.

Book design by Yaffa Jaskoll

americangirl.com/service

ISBN 978-1-338-11506-2

10 9 8 7 6 5 4 3 2 1   18 19 20 21 22

Printed in the U.S.A.   23
First printing 2018

For my mom, Carol Hutton,
a classic American girl

Chapter One

Bzzz!

At the sound of the buzzer on the other side of the room, Caitlin Moore pulled her hand away from her own buzzer and scowled. She hadn't been quite fast enough.

"Ulysses S. Grant's middle name was just the letter 'S,'" answered the captain of the eighth-grade trivia team.

"Correct, Alex," said Mr. Patel, the trivia team adviser. "And that ties the sixth- and eighth-grade teams. This was our final official question, so now we move on to the sudden death bonus round. Whoever scores a point first will win the match."

Caitlin exchanged a nervous look with her teammates: her best friend, Natalia; Natalia's twin sister, Zoe;

and the twins' cousin Emma. They were the sixth-grade champion team, and they had been in the lead for the last several questions, easily passing the now-eliminated seventh-grade team and keeping a point or two ahead of the eighth graders. But they might lose the tournament after all. Natalia gave Caitlin a nervous smile, but Zoe was frowning and Emma's face looked pale and pinched with anxiety.

This is it. Caitlin held her breath as Mr. Patel drew out an index card and looked back and forth between Caitlin and Alex. This was the question that could decide everything.

Breathe, she told herself, and took a deep gulp of air, trying to relax.

"For the win," Mr. Patel said, "what bird is the fastest flier?"

Hummingbird, Caitlin thought, but she was too late. Alex slammed his hand down on the buzzer. Without even conferring with his team, he said confidently, "The hummingbird."

Caitlin's heart sank. The team that won their school's competition would compete with other middle school teams from around the county; the winner of the county competition would compete in the state semifinals; and the winner of the semifinals would compete in the state championship.

And the team that won the state championship would win not only the right to compete in the national championship in New York City, but would also get $250 for each member of the team and another $1,000 for their school library.

The national champions would get more money for their school, money toward college, and, best of all, an all-expenses-paid trip to New York City for them and their families for the whole week of the competition. Caitlin had always wanted to go to New York. But now the eighth graders had won instead, and Caitlin's team wouldn't even go on to the county competition. Tears prickled at the edges of her eyes, and she blinked hard to force them away.

"I'm afraid that's incorrect," Mr. Patel said. "The hummingbird has the fastest heartbeat and beats its wings the most times per second, but it is *not* the fastest flier."

There's still a chance. Quickly, Caitlin pressed her own buzzer.

"Sixth grade," Mr. Patel said.

They had a chance, but what was the answer? Caitlin knew she had learned this fact while she'd been studying—she could almost picture the page in a book on animals that gave the fastest, slowest, biggest, smallest, and so on—but she couldn't remember what it had actually said. She looked to her teammates for an answer.

Zoe gave her a crooked smile and shook her head, her sleek, dark bob swinging past her chin. "No clue," she whispered.

Next to her twin, Natalia was bouncing in her seat. "I bet it's the golden eagle," she said.

Emma was frowning thoughtfully, her hands twisting in her lap. "I'm pretty sure it's the peregrine falcon," she murmured. "But I'm not *totally* sure."

Caitlin bit her lip, trying to make up her mind. She was the captain, so the final choice of answer was hers. Right now, what she picked could snag them the win. But if she got it wrong, Mr. Patel would ask a new question and the eighth-grade team would have another chance to beat them.

Caitlin thought hard, not about the question but about her teammates. Emma was extremely responsible and studied much harder for these competitions than Natalia did, but Natalia *loved* animals. If this wasn't an animal question, Caitlin would go with Emma's answer, no doubt about it. But facts about animals were Natalia's specialty.

Caitlin opened her mouth to give Natalia's answer: golden eagle.

Then she hesitated. Natalia had said that she would *bet* it was the golden eagle. That didn't sound like she knew for sure, just that she thought it was a likely answer. If Emma was *pretty sure* the answer was the peregrine falcon, then she was a lot surer than Natalia was.

"You have five more seconds to give your answer," Mr. Patel told her, looking at the timer in front of him.

"Peregrine falcon," Caitlin blurted, and then held her breath. Had she chosen right?

Mr. Patel paused dramatically before announcing,

"Correct! The sixth-grade team is our school champion! Congratulations, girls!"

Caitlin squealed and leaped to her feet. She and Natalia hugged, and then Emma and Zoe piled in for a four-way group hug. Everyone was applauding, even the defeated seventh- and eighth-grade teams. Caitlin felt light and fizzy with excitement. *This is the first step*, she thought. *We're going to win it all. We're one victory closer to going to New York!*

Fifteen minutes later, Caitlin wriggled impatiently in one of four chairs pulled up in front of Mr. Patel's desk. Usually, Caitlin prided herself on being poised and polite, and paying attention to adults—she liked it when people said how mature she was for her age—but right now she was too excited to sit still.

"Good work, girls," Mr. Patel said, smiling at them. "I'm impressed that you were able to win against the seventh and eighth graders."

Caitlin and Natalia grinned at each other. It *did* make victory a little sweeter that their opponents had all been a little bit older than they were.

"Now the real work begins," Mr. Patel said, pushing up his glasses and looking more serious as he handed them each several papers. "You'll be competing against the champion teams from other schools. Here are permission slips for your parents to sign and guides to what the topics and rules are for the inter-school contests. And you need to officially pick a captain and have her fill out the form with the names and ages of everyone on the team."

"Caitlin's the captain," Natalia said immediately. Caitlin smiled at her best friend. She could always count on Natalia.

"That's up to the four of you," Mr. Patel said. "But fill out the form to make it official for the competition and return it to me by Monday along with the permission slips. You'll have two weeks to study for the county competition."

Only two weeks! Caitlin thought. *We've got a* lot *to do.*

⌒☉

After school, the girls walked home together.

"Winning the trip to New York would be awesome," Natalia said dreamily, pushing a long brown curl out of her face. She flipped through the papers Mr. Patel had given them. "Look, we'd get tickets to a Broadway show for us and our families. And go to the top of the Empire State Building, and take a bus tour of the city, and visit the Metropolitan Museum of Art!"

Caitlin felt a little thrill run through her, but she tried not to get carried away. "*First*, we have to win a whole bunch of competitions before we can start planning our victory trip," she said. "I think we should practice at lunch every day and at least twice a week after school. And on Saturdays and Sundays."

"Zoe and Emma and I help at Seaview House on weekend mornings for brunch," Natalia reminded her. "And Emma has swim meets almost every Saturday. And I have dogs to walk."

"And I have art class on Saturday afternoons," Zoe added.

"Well, can everybody do Sunday afternoons?" Caitlin asked. She pulled out her phone and made a note of everyone's schedules. "And maybe Wednesdays and Fridays after school? I'll email you guys a schedule." Everybody nodded, but Caitlin suddenly felt a stab of worry. What if they didn't want her to be in charge? "I mean, if you still want me to be captain. I don't have to be, if someone else wants to."

Zoe rolled her eyes. "I *definitely* do not want to be captain," she said. "Spending my time organizing everyone else? No, thank you. You're good at it."

"I don't want to be captain, either," Emma said, hitching her backpack higher on her shoulder. "I feel weird enough about being up on a stage with a bunch of strangers looking at us. I'd be too nervous to give the answers in the competitions."

"You'll be fine onstage," Natalia reassured her cousin. "And *you*"—she nudged Caitlin with a friendly elbow—"are a terrific captain. You're definitely the best one of us to do it."

"Thanks," Caitlin said, pleased. "So, the basic schedule sounds okay to you guys?"

"Sure," Natalia said, and the others nodded. "We'll have to study even more before the nationals," she added.

Zoe frowned. "*If* we make the nationals," she said. "Remember, kids from other schools are going to be working really hard, too."

"Definitely. We can't count on winning," Natalia said, but the shine in her eyes made Caitlin sure that, in Natalia's mind, she was already halfway up the Empire State Building.

And Caitlin could imagine it so clearly, too. "Well, why not?" she said. "If we work hard enough, why wouldn't we win?"

⁓

That night, Caitlin looked in satisfaction at a color-coded schedule showing exactly what they'd study when, and a pile of index flash cards in the same colors. The trivia contests would concentrate on five different categories—animals and nature, American history, arts and music, sports, and literature—and she'd assigned a different color to each one. "Green for nature," she murmured to herself, laying out the stack of cards in that color. "Orange for history. Blue for arts and music, pink for sports, and purple for literature."

Each of her friends, she decided, would be responsible for researching certain subjects. They'd all quiz each other on everything, but each would specialize in their specific topics and share what they learned with the others. It would make studying much more efficient.

She could hear the quiet clank of dishes from downstairs as her older brother, Robbie, loaded the dishwasher, and she smiled. Being team captain was already having some benefits. On most nights, she was the one who would have to help clean up after dinner while her brother studied for the SAT or worked on college applications, but her mom had let Caitlin off tonight so that she could start putting her study scheme together. She stretched luxuriously, enjoying being able to focus on her own work instead of chores.

Caitlin neatly stacked the flash cards and copies of the schedule on her desk for tomorrow. Then she climbed into bed and curled up on top of the pink-flowered comforter. It was going to be *awesome*, she thought, traveling to the big city with all her best friends and getting to be the one who gave her whole family an amazing experience like that, too. If she worked together with Natalia, Emma, and Zoe, the four of them could do anything.

Chapter Two

"I'm almost out of blinis," Caitlin told Zoe, holding tightly to the edge of her tray and frowning down at the few little appetizers left on it.

Her friends had drafted her to help serve hors d'oeuvres at today's spring garden party at their family's bed-and-breakfast, Seaview House.

Zoe, Emma, and Natalia helped out at Seaview House every weekend at brunch, bringing people drinks and clearing dishes off the tables, and also handing around trays of appetizers or desserts at weddings and parties. So, *they* had all perfected the art of balancing a heavy tray of food while smiling and walking. But Caitlin discovered this was not as easy as they made it look. She had to balance an awkward, tippy tray to avoid dropping it and strewing pancakes and fish and some kind of cream—and what was that black stuff? caviar?—across the garden. She hadn't expected the weird tiny pancakes with smoked fish on top of them to go so fast—they looked kind of gross to her—but all the guests seemed to love them, and her tray was almost empty.

"Here, I'll switch with you," said Zoe, who had just come out from the kitchens, expertly balancing a full platter of tiny crab cakes. "But first, tell me who our tallest president was."

"Abraham Lincoln," Caitlin said confidently. She hadn't read this fact when she was studying, but she knew Lincoln had been famous for being unusually tall.

"Correct," Zoe said, and passed over the crab cakes, taking Caitlin's almost-empty tray. "I haven't taken crab cakes down by the fountain yet, so maybe try over there? I'll hand these out here and then go get another tray."

"Wait," Caitlin said. "What are the two national sports of Canada?"

"They have more than one?" Zoe asked, shifting the blini tray to one side to balance it against her hip. She looked up as if the answer to Caitlin's question might be written in the sky. "Wow, I hate sports questions. Is one of them ice hockey?"

"Good guess!" Caitlin said. "Ice hockey is their national winter sport. The other one is a summer sport—it's lacrosse." She grinned at Zoe and then, balancing her tray very carefully, took small, level steps toward the stairs to the next part of the garden. Halfway down the staircase, she stepped a little too hard and everything wobbled, but she managed to make it down without a disaster. Caitlin blinked in the bright sunlight as she carried her tray across the second level to where a white fountain bubbled, surrounded by brightly colored tulips and daffodils.

Caitlin's parents were by the fountain, talking with Zoe and Natalia's dad, who taught at the high school. Her dad winked at her and took a crab cake, the skin around his eyes crinkling as he smiled. "You're looking like a professional," he told her, and she stood straighter, wondering if the guests who didn't know her thought she was older than twelve.

Emma came out of the crowd beyond them, her tray of mini tarts half-empty. "Natalia just asked me what the oldest living animal was," she said. "I didn't know, but now I do. Want to guess?"

"Like, the longest living species, or the actual individual animal?" Caitlin asked as she held out her tray to a guest.

"Actual individual animal," Emma said, offering her tray to the guest, too. "I mean, I don't think they can know for sure, can they? But there's an answer for oldest *known* individual animal."

"I have no idea," Caitlin said. A tinge of worry crept into her mind. Zoe hadn't known the Canadian sports question. And neither Emma or Caitlin had known this one. There were just so many facts in the world! How could they learn everything about any category?

"It was a clam named Ming, and it lived to be more than five hundred years old," Emma told her. They looked at each other seriously for a moment, and then the corners of Emma's lips quivered uncontrollably. Caitlin couldn't help giggling.

"Who named the clam?" she asked. "And how did they know it was more than five hundred years old? Five hundred years ago, who was keeping track of clams' ages? Did they write down, 'Today, Ming turned six'? Was he special from the beginning, or were they celebrating every clam's clammiversary?"

"There are so many questions," Emma said, deadpan, and they both dissolved into giggles again before they went off to circulate their appetizers some more.

Natalia was on the lowest level of the garden, carrying a frosty pitcher of lemonade. Her long hair was blowing in all directions, and she had a big grin on her face. She was talking to everybody, moving confidently from one conversation to another. She turned with a happy greeting to fill the glass of someone Caitlin vaguely recognized from around town—"Hey, Mrs. Lau. You didn't bring the baby today?" Natalia always seemed to know everybody, and to get to know new people fast.

As the woman she had been talking to walked away with a glass of lemonade, Natalia spotted Caitlin. "I've got a trivia question for you," she said, and paused dramatically. "What was the animal with the longest recorded life?"

"Ming the clam, of course," Caitlin said matter-of-factly. "Everybody knows that." She turned away from Natalia's surprised face before she let herself smile.

⁓

After the garden party was over and they had helped to clean up, the four girls walked along the shore from Seaview House to the town boardwalk, which had just reopened after being closed all winter. The inland side of the boardwalk had a few small stores and food stands; the other overlooked a small sandy beach and the blue, blue waters of the Chesapeake Bay. Gulls wheeled overhead, screeching.

"I love it when these stores first open for the season," Natalia said. "It means that summer's almost here."

Caitlin sniffed the air, which smelled of French fries from the crab-and-burger stand they were passing. The breeze off the bay that tangled her curls carried the scent of fish and salt water. "I love it, too," she said.

Emma looked fondly from the fudge-and-saltwater-taffy shop to the one that sold T-shirts and bathing suits.

"This'll be my first whole summer in Waverly," she said. "Let's come down here a lot."

"Whole summer?" asked Zoe. "Aren't you going back to Seattle for a couple weeks?"

Emma shrugged. "Yeah, but that's just a visit. I *live* here now."

"And we're glad you do," Natalia said, slinging an arm over her cousin's shoulder.

Caitlin felt a tiny twinge of jealousy. She'd been *really* jealous of Emma's friendship with Natalia when Emma first moved to Waverly, back in the fall. It had felt like Emma was stealing Natalia away from her. But as she'd gotten to know Emma, she'd gotten to like her. Like her a lot, actually, but she still didn't feel she knew Emma as well as she knew Natalia and Zoe—or as well as the other three knew each other. It felt strange sometimes that her three best friends were all family, like she was just a little bit outside their special circle. But Caitlin refused to let that tiny touch of jealousy take root.

"Hey, let's talk about the trivia contest," Caitlin said, leading the way to one of the wooden picnic tables outside the crab shack. The wood was worn smooth with years of use. Once it was fully summer, there would be people holding their fries and waiting for these tables, and they wouldn't be able to sit down unless they bought something, but the boardwalk was empty enough now that no one minded them taking one.

"See," she said, taking copies of the schedule she'd drawn up out of her bag and handing them around, "I've color-coded each general topic. We can concentrate on one of the topics for the first half of each study session, and then we can spend the second part quizzing each other on everything."

There was a long pause as her friends stared at the papers in front of them. Caitlin began to feel a little hot and uncomfortable. Maybe she had scheduled too many study sessions. "I mean, if this is too much . . ." she began.

But Emma was nodding. "No, the plan totally makes sense."

"I like that you chose green for animals and nature," Zoe said, running an artistic eye over the multicolored schedule. "It's very thematic."

"And very thorough!" Natalia added. "This looks

great, Caitlin; I know you put in a lot of work planning it." She gave Caitlin a playful nudge. "Best captain ever. The Queen of Trivia."

Caitlin relaxed. "Yeah?" she asked. "Well, I'm happy to accept you guys as my trivial court."

"Oh, thanks so much," Zoe said, smirking. "I've always wanted to be trivial."

"Excellent," Caitlin said, and straightened out her own copy of the schedule. "So, I thought we should divide up the topics, too. Like, we can all study everything, but one person will be in charge of the research for each topic and be the expert on it. If I'm the Queen of Trivia, Emma can be the Sultan of Sports since she does soccer and swimming. Natalia can be the, um, Knight of Nature since she loves animals."

"And I'll be the Aristocrat of Art, right?" Zoe said. "Does that mean you're planning to be the expert for both literature and American history? That seems like a lot for one person."

"Well, there are five topics and only four of us," Caitlin explained. "And I don't mind doing two. I like literature and history."

The other three girls glanced at each other. "We could all help out," Emma suggested. "We could divide up history by the time period or something so that everybody does just a little bit of it. I wouldn't mind."

Caitlin shook her head, thinking, *I don't need any help.* She was a straight-A student and super-organized; she would do a great job at this. "As long as everybody else does their part, I can handle mine," she said.

"Well, okay," Emma said, shrugging. "If you're sure."

Zoe raised one skeptical eyebrow, but she finally shrugged, too. "If anyone can handle doing twice the work of everyone else, it's you, Caitlin," she said.

Natalia grinned at Caitlin. "All hail the Queen of Trivia!"

～❦～

They hung out on the beach for a while longer, playing chicken with the cold waves, getting as close to the water as possible and then running back away at the last minute. Caitlin made a face and wiggled her freezing toes inside her wet shoes. Her yellow dress was damp and had patches of sand on the hem. The others could walk home from the boardwalk, but Caitlin's house was far enough away that she would need a ride. And her mom *loved* her SUV and hated it when the inside got dirty. "My mom's going to be mad about the wet sand when she picks me up," Caitlin announced.

"Come over to my place," Emma suggested. "You can wear something of mine while you put your stuff through the washing machine."

Hanging out at Emma's for a while and trying on some of her clothes sounded fun. And Emma's dad, who was the chef at the bed-and-breakfast, always had something good to eat in the kitchen. "Okay," Caitlin said. "Thanks." They walked down the shore, picking up seashells and looking for little sand crabs, until they reached Zoe and Natalia's house.

"We'll be thinking of you guys while we're wrangling my little brothers," Natalia said, turning down the walk, and sighed gustily. "We promised my parents we'd babysit the monsters this afternoon."

"Oh, please, you love playing with your brothers," Caitlin said. Natalia was always making up games and stories for Tomás, who was in first grade, and Mateo, who was five. "And Zoe seems to tolerate them pretty well."

"Tolerate is about accurate," Zoe said. "I mean, I love them and everything, but Natalia likes playing LEGO and making fart noises a lot more than I do." She held up her trivia schedule. "Tomorrow is a blue day, so I'll bring everything I can about arts and music."

Caitlin and Emma walked side by side to Seaview House. They hurried quietly through the living room, where a couple bed-and-breakfast guests were gathered, and up several flights of stairs to the attic, where Emma and her parents had their apartment.

"I like your clothes," Caitlin told Emma, flipping through the closet. "They're very you." Caitlin thought privately that they were a little plainer than she liked to wear herself, but Emma's clothes, neat and practical, were nice, too.

Emma's room was blue and white with a slanting ceiling and looked down through a whole row of windows onto the bay. It felt like a cool, airy nest high above the ground. Caitlin looked in the mirror and smoothed down the shirt she'd borrowed, which was a deep lapis-lazuli blue. Looking at her reflection, she caught sight of a familiar flyer behind her on Emma's desk and turned.

"Oh, hey," she said, picking up the flyer. "Are you going to submit something to the literary magazine?"

"I was thinking about it," Emma said, and added, sounding a little shy, "I like to write, sometimes." The editorial board of the school literary magazine was all eighth graders, but anyone in Waverly Middle School could submit to it.

"Me, too," Caitlin told her. "I was going to try to write something, but I decided it was more important to study for the trivia tournament," she continued wistfully. She loved making up stories, and it would have been cool to see her own words in print in the magazine.

"I thought about that, too," Emma said, taking the flyer from Caitlin and studying it. "And then I thought that it would be a nice break when my brain is tired from real-world facts. I might write an actual fantasy story, with magic powers and monsters and stuff."

"And maybe you could even combine some of the facts you learned with the fantasy," Caitlin suggested, a spark of excitement flashing through her. "Like, you'd have the truth about polar bear hibernation if your magical person could talk to animals."

"As we both know, polar bears don't hibernate unless they're pregnant," Emma said, her face dead serious.

"Exactly," Caitlin said. "It's that real-world knowledge that'll make the fantasy feel true."

Emma seemed impressed. "I think you're right," she said. "Hey, do you want to write a story together? It'll be good to have imagination breaks in between study sessions, and it'll be fun." Emma added, "And with two of us working on it, the story will go faster and take less time away from the contest than if just one of us was writing it."

"That's true." Caitlin hesitated: She was the captain—didn't she have a responsibility to work harder than anyone else? But it *did* sound fun. "Maybe we could set it in New York?" she suggested, feeling a flicker of excitement. "That would be a good place for a fantasy. Things could happen in museums and skyscrapers, and we could pretend they have polar bears in the zoo, if we want polar bears in the story."

"I would *love* to set the story in New York," Emma said excitedly. "What if one of the characters can make plants grow by magic? They could come up through the sidewalk and in the lobbies of big apartment buildings, like a jungle in the middle of concrete and asphalt."

"That would be really cool," said Caitlin. "Do you want to start plotting now, while my clothes are getting clean?"

Emma plopped down on one of the large floor pillows near the windows and reached for a notebook. "Let's do it! Can we call the girl Athena? I've always loved that name."

"Sure." Caitlin felt a warm surge of affection toward Emma. It felt good to be creating something unique with her.

Chapter Three

"Um, which composer composed some of his greatest works after becoming totally deaf?" Zoe looked across the table. "Caitlin?"

"Beethoven," Caitlin said, completely sure, and picked up another flash card as Zoe nodded. "Natalia. What dance is known as 'the dance of love'?"

"Uh." Natalia stared up at the cafeteria ceiling, thinking. "Hang on. The tango. No, wait, the rumba! Ruuuummmba!" She wiggled in her seat, arms in the air, pretending to dance.

"Correct!" Caitlin said. "Your turn."

"Okay, Emma." Natalia shuffled through the blue index cards. "Here's one. What is the style of

Neo-Impressionist art that uses tiny dots of colors to form an image?"

Emma bit her lip. There was a long pause. "Point . . . pointillism?" she said at last, sounding unsure.

"That's right!" Natalia cheered. "Good job!"

Caitlin sat up alertly, ready for Emma to ask her another question. They'd made it through three whole rounds of questions without anyone making a mistake. They were so ready for this competition. They were on fire!

～⌒～

THURSDAY, SPORTS, THE CAFETERIA

"Natalia!" Caitlin said sharply. "Did you even hear the question?" Her best friend was staring at their usual lunch table—they'd taken an empty table to study at instead of sitting with their other friends this week— where a bunch of girls were huddled around their friend Vivian, all looking at something on the table and talking excitedly.

"I just want to find out what they're talking about." Natalia said, half rising as the girls around Vivian all suddenly burst into laughter.

"No!" Caitlin stood up and glared at Natalia. "We have to study!"

"Caitlin, calm down," Zoe said.

"Sorry," Caitlin said, taking her seat. "But we have to be serious. We've only got a little more than a week before the county competition. We can't get distracted." She'd been working so *hard*, staying up late looking up trivia about literature and American history. There was so much to both subjects! *I can do it, though*, she reassured herself. *But I need the whole team to work as hard as I do.*

"We've been studying *every* day at lunch," Natalia complained, and absentmindedly bit into her sandwich. She swallowed and went on, "And we studied at your house last night, and we're going to study at our house tomorrow. I don't have any free time anymore."

"It is a lot of practice," Zoe agreed.

"But it'll be worth it, won't it?" Emma asked, looking around at them. "If we do our best, we'll have a chance at winning." Caitlin wanted to hug her. At least Emma understood.

"Come on," Caitlin coaxed. "Just think about that trip

to New York City. Think about being the best trivia team in the whole country."

Natalia sighed. "I guess you're right." She looked at their usual lunch table again, longingly. The girls there were trading desserts now, and Caitlin saw Natalia's hand twitch toward the s'mores brownies Emma had brought them all from her dad. But then she looked away and smiled. "Completely right. Ask me the question again."

"In what country did the game of tennis originate?" Caitlin asked.

Natalia frowned thoughtfully. "France?"

"England," Caitlin corrected her, thinking, *We have to work harder.*

⁓

NEXT WEDNESDAY AFTERNOON, AMERICAN HISTORY, SEAVIEW HOUSE

"I am so tired of this," Zoe said. They were all sitting at the kitchen table in Emma's family's apartment on the top floor of Seaview House. Zoe, resting her chin in one hand, was doodling a picture of herself on a piece of scrap paper with her other hand. Doodle Zoe was facedown, asleep on the table, her short dark hair sticking up in all directions. Zoe added a row of *zzz*'s rising above her.

"Oh, come on," Caitlin said irritably. A dull ache was spreading from the middle of her forehead. She had stayed up late looking up facts about American history, and now she felt grumpy and sleepy. "What was the play Abraham Lincoln and his wife were watching the night he was assassinated?"

"Why are so many of these questions about Abraham Lincoln?" Emma wondered.

"Well, he was important," Caitlin insisted.

Zoe rolled her head back to rest against the top of her chair, her eyes half-shut. "*Our Mutual Friend,*" she said.

"Wrong. It was *Our American Cousin,*" Caitlin said. "Close, though. *Our Mutual Friend* is that Charles Dickens novel that was an answer when we did literature yesterday." She started to pass the stack of orange index cards to Zoe so she could ask the next question, and then paused. "Wait. Where are you going?"

Natalia, who had quietly gotten up from the table and headed for the door, turned around, her smile stiff. "I have two boxers and a dachshund I have to walk," she said.

"*Natalia*," Caitlin said. She could hear that she was whining, and she wasn't proud of it, but there was so much to do! How could Natalia just get up and walk out?

"*Caitlin*," Natalia said back, mimicking her tone. "The B and B guests hired me to walk these dogs. I have to do it. The dogs can't wait forever. They'd ruin the rugs, and I'd get in trouble. And we've been working for ages." Her eyes narrowed. "I think we should be done now." She headed for the door. Zoe laid down her cards on the table and got up and followed her.

"I want to get outside for a while, too," she said. "I'll see you guys later."

Caitlin's head ached even more, and she rubbed her forehead. They had so much still to get through. "I can't believe them," she told Emma. "The county tournament is on Saturday! How do they expect to win if they're not taking it seriously?"

"They're not studying machines," Emma said, looking worried. "And we *have* been working for a really long time. You have to let them take breaks. Encourage them. This is supposed to be fun, right?"

Fun isn't going to get us to New York, Caitlin thought to herself. But after a moment, she sighed and said, "I guess I could use a break." It would be good to think about something else for a while.

"We've got cheesecake in the fridge," Emma said, tempting her. "We could take some and go hang out in my room until Zoe and Natalia come back."

"Do you want to work on the story?" Caitlin asked. They'd been writing it whenever they had free time, sometimes together and sometimes emailing each other ideas and writing. And Emma had been right: When Caitlin's brain was overloaded with trivia, it was good to be able to shut it all down and think about a fantasy kingdom hidden deep in the heart of New York City, and Athena, the girl they'd invented who had the power to make plants grow and could talk to animals.

"I would *love* to work on the story," Emma agreed. "I was thinking, maybe Athena could have a friend she travels with?"

"It's a good idea," Caitlin said. "What if it was, like, a unicorn or something? A magic animal that could help guide her. Or a talking animal that *looks* like a regular animal."

"It might be better if it were a regular person," Emma objected. "If her friend were a boy, we could have a love story."

Caitlin made a face. "Ugh. No. I don't think I could write about love without it sounding silly. And don't you think something like that would slow down the plot?"

Emma thought. "I guess you're right," she said slowly. "But I really think the person she travels with should be a *person*, not something magical. I feel like Athena should be the only magic person in the story. It makes her special."

"Okay," Caitlin said. "I see your point. Athena's companion should be a regular person. It can even be a boy. But no romance."

"Agreed," Emma said. She got up and rummaged in the shining silver refrigerator. "Oh, good, there's lots left." Pulling out a covered pie tin, she set it on the counter and got out a knife.

"Yum," Caitlin said. The cheesecake looked good, with a chocolatey bottom and some kind of strawberry glaze on top. "Do we *have* to share with Natalia and Zoe when they get back? We could just eat it all and hide the evidence," she joked.

Emma grinned. "Unless you eat about six slices while they're walking the dogs, there'll be plenty." She hesitated and then said, "But when they get back, maybe we shouldn't study any more today. We could watch TV or something."

"I guess," Caitlin said. "I suppose it wouldn't hurt to end a little early, just this once."

~ ∞ ~

FRIDAY AFTERNOON, ALL TOPICS, ZOE AND NATALIA'S HOUSE

Caitlin's head was swimming. It was the day before the county championship, and the four girls were at Zoe and Natalia's house after school. They'd been quizzing each other for hours, the different colored index cards mixed together so that they got all five kinds of questions randomly, just as they would in competition.

While she usually liked the comfortable chaos and noise of Zoe and Natalia's house, right now all the different sounds were driving her up the wall. Mateo and Tomás were chasing each other up and down the stairs, shouting. "Wild wolf pack, gather!" Mateo screeched, and Tomás squealed with laughter. A Spanish-language radio station was playing, and Caitlin could hear the buzz of adult conversation from the living room downstairs.

Natalia flopped back down on her bed and threw her arm across her eyes. "I'm dead," she said. "I was killed by literature."

From her seat on the floor, Caitlin eyed the stack of index cards. They'd gone through a lot of them, but there was still so much left to review. "The county tournament is *tomorrow*, so we don't want to be unprepared!" she told the others. "Losing the first time we play other teams would be awful."

"But we've been studying *forever*," Natalia said.

Zoe was sitting at her desk, twirling a pencil between her fingers. "I'm not learning anything anymore. My brain has shut off."

Caitlin looked at Emma, sitting on the floor with her back against Zoe's bed. Over the last two weeks, she'd found herself turning to Emma with anything that needed to be decided—schedule questions or what to study when or how to get Zoe and (especially) Natalia to cooperate. Sometimes it seemed as if Emma was the only other one taking their preparation seriously enough.

Emma met her gaze. "Sometimes a good captain has to know when to hold off so the team doesn't burn out before the game," she said.

"If that's a sports metaphor, I'm not listening!" Natalia shouted, and pulled a pillow over her head. "My brain has overdosed on sports!"

"Okay, I guess we can stop," Caitlin said. She pulled the cards toward her and started stacking them neatly. "But tomorrow morning, look over your subject areas first thing."

"Relax," Zoe told her. "We know the plan."

"What should we do now?" Emma asked. "I don't have to be home for another hour."

"Ooh, I know," Natalia said, shoving the pillow aside and sitting up with new energy. "Do you guys know how to play MASH? Vivian showed me."

"Is this what you guys got in trouble for doing during algebra?" Zoe asked.

Natalia rolled her eyes. "Teachers have no sense of humor." She pulled out a piece of scrap paper. "Okay, it stands for Mansion, Apartment, Shack, House," she said, writing the words at the top of the paper. "And we write down some other stuff—jobs or pets you might have, cities you might live in, and someone you might marry."

"I want a pet raccoon," Zoe said, craning to look at the paper.

"This is for Caitlin," Natalia said. "And Caitlin doesn't want a raccoon."

"What do I get?" Caitlin said, trying to see the paper, too.

"Only fate can decide that," Natalia said, shielding the paper as she wrote. "Okay," she said after a few minutes. "Pick a number."

"Five," Caitlin said.

"Okay. One, two, three, four, five," Caitlin said, going over the paper and crossing off the fifth item on the list. "One, two, three, four, five. One, two, three, four, five."

She went back and forth until she'd gotten everything except one option in each category crossed off. Then she said, "Okay, Caitlin. You're going to live in a mansion. In Hawaii."

"Hooray!" Caitlin said.

"You'll be a dog trainer and have six kids."

"I guess I could use the space I have in my huge mansion, then," Caitlin responded.

"And you'll have a pet elephant." Natalia grinned. "It'll entertain the children. Ooh, and you'll be married to Nathan."

Nathan was a boy in their class who never stopped talking. "Do I have to?" Caitlin asked.

Natalia shrugged. "Fate has spoken."

"Ugh." Caitlin leaned back against the wall, watching Natalia as she began on another MASH, this one for Emma. For the past few days, they'd been getting on each other's nerves—Natalia had gotten less and less cooperative about studying as much as Caitlin thought they needed to, and Caitlin knew Natalia thought she was being too bossy. But now this silly game was reminding Caitlin why she liked Natalia so much. Natalia was always ready to do something fun.

I have to remember, Caitlin thought, *even though I want to win, our friendship is more important.*

Still, I really do hope we win!

Chapter Four

"The Louisiana Purchase was in 1803, when the US doubled its size by buying eight hundred and twenty-eight million square miles of territory from France," Caitlin muttered, pressing her hands against her temples as if she could squeeze the information into her brain. "The blue whale makes the loudest sound of any animal."

Zoe turned around in the minivan's middle row of seats to stare at her. "Relax, Caitlin! We're going to be fine," she said.

Zoe's mother, who was driving, glanced into the rear-view mirror at them. "Zoe, if you can turn around like that, your seat belt isn't on properly," she said. "Please fix it."

Zoe subsided back into her seat. From the seat next to Zoe, Emma said, "It'll be fine. We've prepared as much as anyone could." Her voice took on a nervous note. "I'm just glad *I* don't have to be the one to give the team answers."

Caitlin groaned and pressed her hands harder against her head. She wasn't usually shy, but right now the idea of being the spokesperson for her team in front of a whole bunch of strangers sounded awful. What if they couldn't answer a single question? What if they'd studied all the wrong things?

"It's going to be fun," Natalia said from the seat beside her. Unlike everyone else, she looked happy and excited, bouncing in her seat as her mom made the turn into the high school's drive. "Look, there's Mr. Patel waiting for us."

"I'll drop you girls off here, then, and find seats for me and the rest of our families in the auditorium after I park," Natalia and Zoe's mom told them. "Good luck! Break a leg!"

Caitlin took a deep breath. "We're going to be

amazing," she said firmly, like she was swearing an oath. "We're going to win."

"Darn right we are." Natalia flung open the van's sliding door and scrambled out, the others following. "Hey, Mr. Patel!"

"Hi, girls!" Mr. Patel held the door wide for them. "Let's find the auditorium and check in." Inside the auditorium, there was an excited buzz of conversation as teams of middle schoolers and their advisers milled around. "You girls stake out some seats—the first five rows are for competitors—and Caitlin and I will go find out the plan," Mr. Patel said, and Caitlin followed him toward a long table set up in front of the stage.

"Waverly Middle School?" asked the woman behind the table, handing Mr. Patel a clipboard. "I'm Ms. Morgan. We'll need you to fill this out." Smiling at Caitlin, she explained, "We've got eight county middle schools participating, so we'll have three rounds. The four winners of the first round will move on to the second, and then the two winners of the second round will compete for the county championship." She checked her list. "Your team will be in the second match of the first round, against Chestertown Middle School. Each of the matches is twenty questions, and then sudden death in case of a tie."

"Thanks," Caitlin said, fixing a smile on her face. They'd have to sit through a whole match before their own team got up on stage. Was that good or bad? She didn't want to go up on the stage right *now*, but she also felt like she was going to get more and more nervous the longer she had to wait. *At least we can keep studying*, she thought to herself.

As if she knew what Caitlin was thinking, Ms. Morgan added brightly, "And we expect all the teams to pay polite attention while they're waiting to compete."

"Of course," Caitlin answered. *Well, at least we can check out the competition.*

She and Mr. Patel had just made it back to their seats with the other girls when the auditorium doors opened and the audience—parents and friends of the members of all eight teams—streamed in, laughing and talking.

"There are so many people," Emma whispered, sinking down in her seat.

Caitlin could sense hundreds of eyes on the back of her head. She risked glancing over her shoulder. "Nobody's looking at us. Oh, except for our own families." Her parents and Robbie were there, along with Emma's parents and her grandmother, and the twins' parents, their abuelita, and Tomás and Mateo, already squirming impatiently. Tomás waved at her, and she wiggled her fingers back at him.

The audience took their seats, and Caitlin turned back around to face front as the first two teams walked out onto the stage and sat down behind long tables, a buzzer in front of each captain. Ms. Morgan followed them out and explained how the tournament would work. She ended with "We'll begin with the teams from St. Ursula's and Glen Cove Middle School," and the audience applauded.

Caitlin knew St. Ursula's was an all-girls Catholic school in a town about twenty minutes from Waverly. Their captain was a thin, intense-looking blond girl, and all four girls on the team looked confident.

Glen Cove was a public school on the other side of the district. Caitlin was pretty sure that Emma had played them in soccer. There were three boys and a girl on their team. As Caitlin watched, one of the boys said something quietly to the girl. They both laughed, and then straightened up attentively, their eyes on Ms. Morgan.

"First question," Ms. Morgan said. "Who shot Alexander Hamilton?" Caitlin and her teammates exchanged glances. They all knew this one. Zoe, who loved musicals, had been obsessed with *Hamilton* for ages.

Zoe hummed a few bars under her breath.

Before the boy captaining the Glen Cove team had even moved his hand, the intense-looking girl who was the captain of the St. Ursula's team had slammed her hand down on the buzzer. *Bzzz!*

"St. Ursula's," Ms. Morgan called on them.

"Aaron Burr," the blond girl said confidently.

"Correct," Ms. Morgan said.

St. Ursula's took an early lead and, although Glen Cove managed to score a few points, the girls from

St. Ursula's won easily. Caitlin was so interested in their match that she almost forgot her own team was up next—until the audience broke into applause, and the kids from St. Ursula's and Glen Cove got up and left the stage.

"Next, we have Waverly Middle School versus Chestertown Middle School," Ms. Morgan announced, and suddenly, Caitlin couldn't breathe. She sat frozen for a moment before Natalia nudged her. Then they were up on stage, sitting across from the other team— two boys and two girls, all of them wearing matching T-shirts that said *Chestertown Trivia* on them.

"First question," Ms. Morgan said. "What genre of literature did Agatha Christie write?"

Caitlin hit the buzzer a second before the captain of the other team did. "Mystery," she said. *We got lucky. That was an easy one.*

The rest of the match was mostly a blur. Natalia gave Caitlin the wrong answer about where hamsters were first discovered in the wild (Syria, but Natalia thought it was Greece), and Zoe mixed up Monet and Manet, two French painters, but they won.

Caitlin's heart was pounding hard as they filed back off the stage. "We did it," she whispered to the others. "The first step. New York, here we come!"

"Start spreading the news!" Natalia sang, a little too loudly, and Zoe shushed her. A soft laugh swept through the audience behind them.

There were two more competitions to sit through before intermission, and then they'd compete again in the second round. Caitlin shifted in her seat, crossing and uncrossing her legs. She felt restless and on edge, uncomfortable in her own skin. Now that they'd won one match, it was even harder to wait for the next.

She tried to watch the teams onstage, and then gave up. "I'm going to the bathroom," she whispered, and Natalia got up to let her out.

In the bathroom, Caitlin washed her hands slowly, killing time.

Emma pushed the door open and came in. "Hey," she said. "You okay? You've been gone a long time."

"Yeah," Caitlin said, drying her hands. "What's going on in there?"

Emma leaned against the sink. "It's a lot closer than ours or the one before ours. Both teams are pretty good."

"I guess we should get back in there," Caitlin said. They both stayed where they were. "I just couldn't concentrate when I was in there!" Caitlin confessed. "But I know I should be checking out the other teams."

"It's okay to take a break once in a while," Emma told her. "It's like when I'm training for a swim meet: Sometimes it's better to swim really hard for a little while and then take a few minutes to rest, instead of swimming for a long time. The breaks are part of the plan."

"I guess," Caitlin said, biting her lip.

Emma's eyes were sympathetic, as if she understood how Caitlin felt. "I was thinking," she said suddenly, "you know how Athena can talk to animals? What if we changed the beginning of the story to be about when she first started developing the power, and she has to learn to control it?"

Caitlin thought. "Like, at first she's just attracting stray cats and pigeons and stuff? That could be cool."

"Definitely." Emma looked pensive. "What other animals might be loose in New York City?"

"If we win the trip," Caitlin said, "we could do some research. There's a zoo in Central Park. Would it be too Harry Potter if she talked to animals in the zoo?"

The door opened, and Natalia came in. "You guys have been gone *forever*," she said. "What are you doing? I heard you say something about a zoo?"

"We're just taking a break from watching the tournament," Emma told her.

"Well, we'd better head back soon, because the last two teams just went up, and soon it'll be time for the second round," Natalia told them.

"Which team won the last match?" Caitlin asked, wishing she had paid more attention to the differences between the two teams.

But Natalia waved the question away. "I don't remember," she said. "We'll find out in the next round. What were you guys saying about zoos?"

"Oh." Caitlin fiddled with her headband, feeling a little self-conscious. "We're writing a story together to submit to the school literary magazine. And we might have part of it happen in the zoo."

"You guys are writing a story together?" Natalia said. "Huh. Do you want me to read it or anything?"

Caitlin and Emma both stared at her. "You hate reading," Caitlin said.

Natalia made a face. "I don't like reading for *school*," she said. "I'm sure I'd like a story you two wrote. And anyway"—she made a face that was sort of joking, sort of not joking at all—"I hate being left out *way* more."

⁓

When they got back into the auditorium, the last match of the first round was almost over. The kids from Longbranch Middle School—three boys and a girl—were winning easily, more than five points ahead with only a couple questions left to go.

Caitlin focused on those last questions, taking note of what was asked and how the team decided on their answers. The captain was a tall Asian boy with really short hair, and he took the time to listen to each of his teammates on every question before he answered. *He seems like a good captain*, she thought. The more together the other team was, the harder they'd be to beat.

Finally, Ms. Morgan asked the final question. "What was the pen name of the writer Samuel Clemens?"

"Mark Twain," the short-haired captain said immediately.

"Correct! Congratulations, Longbranch Middle School," Ms. Morgan said, and the audience applauded. "We'll be taking a fifteen-minute break now, and then moving on to the second round."

As a lot of the audience filed out to stretch their legs or use the bathroom, Caitlin turned in her seat to talk to the other girls. "Okay, what do we know about the rest of the teams?" she asked.

"The girl on that team that just won really knows her stuff with the art questions," Zoe said quietly, and Caitlin nodded.

"And the captain checks in with everybody," she added. "They're really together."

"St. Ursula's did best in the first round, though," Emma pointed out. "They all seem super-focused. And their match wasn't even close."

"Yeah," Natalia said, twirling a piece of hair nervously around her finger. "I hope we don't go up against them in the second round."

"We can beat them," Caitlin said automatically, but she wasn't feeling quite as confident about it as she sounded. *Can we really?*

Once the break ended and everyone had returned to their seats, Ms. Morgan walked out onto the stage again. "And now we begin the second round," she said. "Our first competitors will be the teams from Waverly Middle School and Longbranch Middle School."

Oh. Caitlin's stomach twisted a little as the team they had just watched win headed for the stage, led by their tall captain. They had been *really* good. "We can do this," she muttered.

"Of course we can, Trivia Queen," Natalia murmured back, bumping their shoulders together. Emma and Zoe nodded, their faces firm with determination.

"First question," Ms. Morgan said once they were all seated onstage. "Who was the only president to remain unmarried throughout his time in the White House?"

I know this. Caitlin jumped out of her seat to slam her hand down on the buzzer before the other team could.

"Waverly Middle School."

"James Buchanan," Caitlin said, breathless.

"Correct," Ms. Morgan announced, and Natalia gave a muted cheer beside her.

And they were off. The other team was sharp and quick and had obviously studied hard, too, but Caitlin's team held their own. Caitlin and the other team's captain both lunged for their buzzers with every question. As they got closer to the end, the teams were neck and neck, one getting a point and then the other, taking turns being a point ahead.

Their rhythm broke on a nature question. Caitlin had already pressed the buzzer and turned to Natalia for an answer.

"I don't remember!" Natalia whispered, her eyes wide and panicked.

"You had that book on volcanoes!" Caitlin whispered back, trying not to get mad. "Did you read it?"

"Kind of!"

"It seems like a pretty basic fact!" Caitlin's face felt hot. Natalia had *promised* she'd look over the books Caitlin had found for her.

"I'm sorry, Waverly, your time is up," Ms. Morgan broke in. "Longbranch, do you have an answer?"

Longbranch's captain hit his buzzer. "Australia is the only continent with no current volcanic activity," he said confidently. Caitlin groaned and then sat up straighter, her eyes on Ms. Morgan, her hand poised for the buzzer. *We're not going to lose!*

By the fifteenth question, they were two points ahead, when Zoe answered incorrectly that the artist famous for his mobiles was Mark Rothko. Longbranch knew the answer was Alexander Calder and got the point. Caitlin gritted her teeth. If they lost one more point, they'd lose their lead. If they lost two, they might lose the whole match.

Energy zinging through her, Caitlin got even faster with the buzzer, so that Waverly got to answer first on every question. Emma was a rock, answering question after question, even though only one sports question came up. The last question came with Waverly comfortably three points ahead.

"Congratulations, Waverly Middle School," Ms. Morgan said, and Caitlin only vaguely heard the applause as she staggered off the stage and collapsed into her seat in the auditorium, accepting a high five from Mr. Patel.

One more round. One more team to beat and we'll be the county champions.

"That was so great! I can't believe it!" Natalia whispered, grabbing Caitlin's hand and squeezing it. The last two teams were going up on stage. "I bet we'll be up against St. Ursula's in the finals."

Caitlin nodded, eyeing the teams onstage. She hadn't seen the other team—also a private school—compete in the first round, but they'd have to be pretty amazing to beat the girls from St. Ursula's. "They're tough," she agreed, and then added, keeping her voice casual, "You really need to concentrate more in the final round."

Natalia paused. "*I* need to concentrate in the last round?" she whispered at last. "Specifically me?"

Caitlin turned to look at her. Natalia was frowning, her dark eyes wary. "Well, you and Zoe," Caitlin whispered back. On the other side of Natalia, Zoe stiffened. "You guys were making a lot of mistakes this last round. Emma and I were the ones who kept us from losing to Longbranch."

Emma leaned forward in her seat to see everyone. "I don't think—"

"Shh! Settle down, girls!" Mr. Patel interrupted from the end of the aisle.

Caitlin faced the stage again. Out of the corner of her eye, she saw Natalia cross her arms and slump down in her seat and couldn't help feeling a tiny bit guilty. *Maybe I could have said that more nicely*, she thought. *But it was true.* She shook her head, focusing back on the competition onstage.

St. Ursula's, as Caitlin had expected, won their round. There was another short break, during which Caitlin and her teammates flipped through their study cards.

Caitlin couldn't help being very aware of the stiff silence of Natalia beside her, glaring down at her cards. *Maybe being mad at me will make her do her best*, Caitlin thought to herself. *She has to learn that she can't just keep fooling around, not if she wants us to win.*

Up on stage, Caitlin only half heard Ms. Morgan welcoming everyone back for the final round. Instead, she was watching St. Ursula's team. Did they look a little tired? Their blond captain's hand was almost on top of their buzzer, and Caitlin moved her own hand closer to hers, hovering directly over it. Every tiny advantage mattered.

The questions came fast, and Caitlin was almost leaping out of her seat to ring the buzzer first. Natalia correctly identified the cause of thunder (the sudden change in air temperature and pressure caused by lightning), Zoe knew the name of the female American impressionist painter famous for painting mothers and children (Mary Cassatt), and Emma could name the football team with the most Super Bowl victories (the Pittsburgh Steelers). Caitlin felt supercharged, lunging for the buzzer and snapping out answers faster than ever before.

When it was time for the last question, they were ahead by a single point. *We have to get this one*, Caitlin thought, leaning forward tensely, her hand as close as possible to the buzzer. *If they get the point, we'll have to go to sudden death. And I don't know how long we can keep this going.*

Ms. Morgan looked at her card and then asked, "What was the name of the individual longest-lived known animal?"

Bzzz! Caitlin brought down her hand and rang the buzzer a fraction of a second before the St. Ursula's captain.

"Waverly Middle School," Ms. Morgan said.

Caitlin's mind went blank. She *knew* this. It was a clam, wasn't it? Or a crab? She remembered laughing about it with Emma at Seaview House's garden party. "I don't know!" she whispered frantically to her team.

They stared back at her for a moment, shocked.

"I don't . . ." Caitlin felt like her brain had completely locked up. Her heart was pounding and her mouth was dry.

"Five seconds, Waverly," Ms. Morgan said. Caitlin could see the St. Ursula's captain poised over her buzzer.

"Ming the clam!" Natalia hissed.

Caitlin's brain snapped back into gear. "Ming the clam!" she almost shouted.

"Correct!" Ms. Morgan smiled. "Congratulations to Waverly Middle School, our county champions!"

The audience burst into applause. Caitlin collapsed back into her seat, breathing hard.

I can't believe I almost lost us the competition.

⁂

Afterward, Mr. Patel took the four of them out for ice cream to celebrate.

"Congratulations, girls," he said, smiling around at them. "I'm so proud of how hard you've worked. I hope you're proud of yourselves, too."

"Oh, we are!" Natalia said cheerfully, digging into her chocolate-raspberry sundae. "I can't believe we managed to beat those St. Ursula's girls. They were *fierce*."

Zoe grinned. "Natalia's obsession with weird animal facts finally paid off."

Emma nodded. "I didn't really expect to be county champions," she confessed. "We were awesome."

Caitlin took a bite of her strawberry ice cream and swallowed hard. Her stomach was a miserable knot of embarrassment. "Thanks for saving me, Natalia," she said quietly. "I can't believe I forgot Ming the clam. I *studied* that fact. I even learned about how scientists dated it using the growth rings on its shell!"

Natalia shrugged. "We're a *team*. I'm glad I knew the answer, though."

Caitlin scraped her spoon through the ice cream. "And I'm sorry I snapped at you about focusing harder," she went on. "You had it more together than I did in the end."

Slinging her arm around Caitlin's neck, Natalia pulled her across the booth's seat and into an awkward half hug. "Don't worry, Trivia Queen," she said. "I probably did need to concentrate more."

"Next stop, the state semifinals," said Emma. "Eeek!"

Chapter Five

MONDAY, HISTORY, THE CAFETERIA

"Okay, Natalia, where was the first permanent English settlement in America founded?" Caitlin rubbed one hand across her tired eyes. She'd sat up late the night before making more flash cards for literature and American history.

"I don't know." Natalia frowned. "Plymouth Rock?"

"Jamestown, Virginia," Caitlin said, and shoved the deck across the table to her.

"Zoe. What were the original thirteen colonies?" Natalia read off the card.

"Maryland," Zoe said. "Massachusetts. New York. Um. Vermont?" She paused, frowning. "I can't remember. Virginia."

Caitlin smiled, tired but determined. "Natalia, read the sentence at the bottom of the card."

Raising her eyebrows skeptically, Natalia read, *"My Nice New Car Needs Re-Painting. Maybe Dark Violet? No, Shiny Gold."* She eyed Caitlin. "Did you go crazy overnight?"

"I think dark violet might actually be a very cool color for a car," Zoe interjected. "Not shiny gold, though."

Emma cocked her head to one side, thinking. "Say the sentence again, slower." Natalia said it again, and Emma smiled. *"My Nice New Car Needs Re-Painting.* Maine, New Hampshire, New York, Connecticut, New Jersey, Rhode Island, Pennsylvania, right? *Maybe Dark Violet.* Massachusetts, Delaware, Virginia. It's a trick to remember the thirteen colonies."

"Ohhhh." Natalia drew out the word, looking impressed. "What's 'Shiny'? I can't even think of a state that starts with 'S.'"

"South Carolina," Caitlin told her. "No, Shiny Gold: North Carolina, South Carolina, Georgia. Get it?"

"That's really clever," Emma said approvingly, and Caitlin felt pleased.

"There's a bunch of different acronyms and tricks to help remember stuff," she said. "I think we can learn a lot before Saturday."

⟨⟨◦⟩⟩

WEDNESDAY, SPORTS, CAITLIN'S HOUSE

"It's the US, right?" Caitlin asked, spreading almond butter on a bagel. Her mom had brought up high-protein brain-food snacks to help them with their studying.

"No, actually," Zoe said, reaching for some edamame. "Try again."

Caitlin frowned at her. "We don't have time to play guessing games, Zoe. Just tell me the answer and we'll move on to the next question."

Zoe rolled her eyes. "Fine, Trivia Queen." The nickname didn't sound so affectionate to Caitlin anymore. "Norway has won the most Winter Olympic medals." She handed Caitlin the pack of question cards.

Natalia closed her eyes and flopped back dramatically to land on Caitlin's pink-and-purple carpet. "No . . . more . . . sports . . ." She sighed.

"Natalia, the next question is yours," Caitlin told her, keeping her voice level and patient. *As captain*, she reminded herself, *it's my job to keep everybody happy and working as a team.*

Natalia groaned. "We studied sports all through lunch and now we've been working for an hour after school, too. I can't take it anymore. My brain is full. You guys even made me learn the rules for *volleyball*."

"You've learned like three volleyball terms; you still don't know how to play," Emma pointed out.

"And I'm proud of it," Natalia retorted. "I am *not* an organized-sports person."

I need to keep the team working together, Caitlin thought, looking down at Natalia, who had now rolled over and was sprawled facedown on the carpet.

"Natalia," Caitlin said, forcing her mouth into a smile. Her face felt stiff with the effort. "Don't you want to win?"

"I guess," Natalia said, rolling onto her back again to look at Caitlin. "But don't you think there's a certain amount of luck to the whole thing? I mean, there's no way anyone can learn everything about all these subjects, so we just learn what we can and hope that the people running the contest pick the questions we studied."

"Yeah," Zoe said, resting her chin on her hand. "So?"

"So, we don't have to go *crazy* with the studying," Natalia said. "We're just stressing ourselves out when it's going to come down to luck in the end."

Caitlin felt like the floor was giving out under her feet. "Actually," she said, "I thought we could start working every day after school this week. Like Natalia says, there's an awful lot to learn."

Natalia sat up and stared at her. Zoe was frowning.

"Working that hard is just going to make me so nervous I forget everything I *do* know," Natalia said stubbornly.

"Look, I want to win and everything, but I'm not going to give up my whole *life*," Zoe chimed in.

Caitlin took a deep breath. She noticed her hands were shaking and pressed them together to keep them still. "You *committed* to this," she said. "Do either of you really want to be the reason we lose?"

"Maybe we should all take a break," Emma said abruptly.

"Instead of round-robining the trivia questions, let's make it a contest," Caitlin suggested. "I'll read out the questions and you guys see who can answer first."

"Okay, shoot," Emma said, leaning forward intensely. Natalia and Zoe exchanged a look.

"What?" Caitlin said.

"Nothing," Zoe said, shrugging. "Sure, let's try that. But we need to stop by four thirty."

"Four *thirty*?" Caitlin said, appalled. "That's only an hour from now! The state semifinals are on Saturday. This is the last chance we have to review literature."

"We can review on our own, too, and we promise we will," Emma said soothingly. "We've studied really hard, Caitlin. We're ready for Saturday."

"Fine," Caitlin said. She flipped over the first card and looked around Emma's family's kitchen table at her friends. Emma was poised on the edge of her seat, ready for the first question. Zoe was leaning back in her chair, her eyes narrowed and fixed on Caitlin. She didn't look as alert as Emma, but she looked ready. Natalia was gazing down at the table, examining her fingernails.

"Okay." Caitlin read off the card. "What was Lewis Carroll's real name?"

"Charles Dodgson," Emma said immediately.

"Good." Caitlin flipped to the next card. "What was Jane Austen's first published novel?"

"*Pride and Prejudice*?" Emma asked.

"Nope; does anyone have another answer?" Caitlin looked around the table. Natalia was still avoiding her eye.

"*Sense and Sensibility*?" Zoe guessed.

"Correct." Caitlin looked at the next card. "What novel by Harper Lee, published in 1960, won the Pulitzer Prize?"

"Ooh, I know," Zoe said. "*To Kill a Mockingbird*. We'll read that in English next year."

"Good." Caitlin picked up the next card but hesitated, looking at Natalia again. Natalia was gazing out the kitchen window, her eyes on the blue water of the bay at the bottom of the hill below. She looked like she was lost in a daydream. Irritation prickled up Caitlin's spine. "Natalia," she said sharply. "Are you even listening?"

"What?" Natalia turned slowly back to the table, blinking as if she'd just woken up.

Annoyance forced the words out of Caitlin's mouth before she could stop them. "You're not even *trying*, are you?"

Natalia frowned. "Excuse me?"

"You're not paying attention. You're not doing the research even when I *hand* you books about the subject *you're* in charge of!"

"That's not fair," Zoe said, bristling. "Natalia's been practicing. *You're* just unreasonable. You want us to only think about the trivia contest all the time."

"This used to be fun," Natalia agreed. "All you do is boss us around now."

"I'm *trying* to make sure we win," Caitlin said. She realized her voice had gotten louder and angrier so that she was almost yelling. She tried to lower it, but when she spoke, her words came out hissing and nasty. "Maybe instead of being snotty, you could step up and—"

"Whatever," Natalia interrupted. Her eyes were shining with tears. She got up, her chair scraping noisily across the kitchen floor. Wiping her eyes angrily, she hurried away from them and out of the apartment, slamming the door behind her. A moment later, they could hear her feet thudding quickly down the stairs.

"Real nice, Caitlin," Zoe said, glaring at her. She got up and followed her twin.

The silence in the apartment after Zoe closed the door behind her was terrible. Caitlin buried her face in her hands. "Ugh!" she half shouted. "Why do they have to be so unreasonable?"

Emma didn't answer. Caitlin drew her hands away and looked up at her friend. Emma was biting her lip and frowning.

"What?" Caitlin asked defensively. "Did you want to say something to me?"

Emma took a deep breath. "I don't think you're being fair to Natalia," she said.

She looked so sincerely sorry as she said it that Caitlin felt her own anger collapsing like a deflated balloon.

"I didn't mean to make Natalia cry," she said. "But I feel like she's not really trying."

"She *is* trying," Emma said. "We've all been working and studying. But these last few weeks, ever since the county competition, you've been pushing everyone way too hard. You're making the practices longer and longer and adding more and more of them. And you get mad whenever anyone says it's too much." She hesitated for a second, and then added, "I think you've gotten really competitive and forgotten what's most important on a team."

Caitlin felt her own shoulders slump. "What's most important?" she asked, her voice small.

"The team." Emma pushed her hair away from her face. "We *all* have to win together. Right now, you're acting like you're the boss, but that's not what a captain is. You have to bring out the best in everybody."

"But isn't that what I'm doing? Getting everyone to study as much as they can so we can be the best?" Caitlin said.

"That's not exactly what I mean," Emma said. "Sometimes it's better to listen to people and let them play to their strengths."

"Hmm." Caitlin felt tired. *Emma's right*, she realized. *I haven't been bringing out the best in anybody, I've just been pushing as hard as I can because I really want to win. Maybe I'm not being fair to my team.* She stood up from the table. "You're right," she said. "Do you want to help me find Natalia and Zoe?"

After looking through the upper gardens and by the bay, they finally found the twins down in the lowest level of the garden, sitting on a bench in the middle of the gazebo, talking quietly. As Caitlin and Emma came in, Zoe crossed her arms defensively over her chest and glared at Caitlin, but Natalia looked up and gave her a watery half smile. She wasn't crying anymore, but the rims of her eyes were pink, as if she'd only stopped very recently.

Caitlin felt awful. "I'm sorry," she said.

"You should be," Zoe muttered. *She's looking out for her sister*, Caitlin knew. One thing that had always been true about Zoe and Natalia—even back in kindergarten— was that they both got mad if they thought someone was picking on their sister.

Caitlin turned a little to include Zoe in the apology, too. "I'm sorry. I know I've been pushing too hard and bossing all of you around."

"Maybe you just got carried away?" Natalia suggested. "I know you really like winning." She gave a snort of half-teary laughter.

"Yeah, I do," Caitlin admitted, sitting down on the bench beside Natalia. "But also, I was freaked out because I froze and almost lost us the county competition. I let you guys down, and I wanted to make up for it."

"That's ridiculous," Natalia said, leaning against Caitlin for a second. The warmth of her side was comforting. "You didn't let us down. You might have frozen up on one question, but you answered, like, a *million* right. We couldn't have won without you." Emma and Zoe both nodded in agreement.

"Thanks." Caitlin felt like Natalia's words were soothing a raw place inside her. Looking around at her friends, she forced herself to go on. "Freaking out about missing the question isn't an excuse for being mean to you guys, though." She swallowed. "If you want to choose a different captain, I'll understand."

Natalia's eyes widened and she stared at Caitlin. "Change captains?"

Zoe gave a short laugh. "No way, Caitlin. You're our captain."

"You're a good captain," Natalia agreed. "We just want you to take it a little easier on us."

"And on yourself," said Emma, sitting down on Caitlin's other side. "Maybe we can figure out a schedule that lets us practice enough without totally taking over our lives. And maybe we can help you with your specialties. You're doing twice as much research as everyone else."

Caitlin usually hated anybody thinking she needed help. But her head ached and her eyes were gritty with tiredness. Right now, there was nothing better than knowing her friends had her back.

Chapter Six

Instead of being held at a high school like the county tournament, the state semifinals were at a community center an hour away from Waverly, in Annapolis.

"Look," Natalia said, peering out the van window at the Maryland State House as they drove by. "It's so pretty." The state house had a dome and a portico with tall white columns. It looked fancy and dignified, like something out of an old movie.

"It's the oldest state capitol building still in use," Caitlin told them. "It goes back to 1772."

The other girls looked at her and grinned. "Go, Trivia Queen," Zoe said.

"Oh my gosh," Emma said, her fingers twisting nervously together as they pulled up outside the community center. The parking lot was packed, and groups of kids and their families and advisers were hurrying up the steps to the entrance. "There's so many people here."

"Well, there's—what? Twenty-four counties in Maryland?" Zoe said, glancing at Caitlin for confirmation. When Caitlin nodded, she went on, "So there's twelve teams here at the semifinals."

"And the top three will go on to the finals to compete against the top three from the other side of the state," Caitlin said. She grinned. "We're definitely going to be in the top three, right?"

"Right!" the other girls chorused as Caitlin reached out for a high five from each of them.

"Okay," Zoe and Natalia's mom said. "See you in there, girls!"

Caitlin stepped out of the van and stood shoulder to shoulder with her teammates, peering up at the concrete front of the community center. Now that they were actually here, she felt energy thrumming through her. "We're going to *dominate*."

❧

Caitlin realized that it was a good thing that three of the teams would move on to the state finals. They didn't have to beat *every* other team—not yet anyway—*and* they only had to compete in two rounds. In the first round, the twelve competing teams would be cut down to six. In the second, they would be cut down to the final three.

Caitlin felt even sharper and more focused than she had in the county competition. *Getting enough sleep is helpful*, she thought. *Who knew?* Since they'd moved to their new study schedule for the last two days before the competition—only studying for *half* the lunch period, not meeting *every* day after school, and splitting the history research up so that everyone was in charge of exactly one and a quarter categories—she'd been feeling more relaxed.

She and Emma had even had time to plot the ending to their Athena story, in which an eagle swooped down and rescued her from the top of the Empire State Building as long, clinging vines growing up the building's sides pulled the bad guys down before they could grab her. It was very exciting, they thought, and when they let Natalia read it, she had agreed. "If the reading we had to do for school had more talking animals and plants attacking villains, I would enjoy reading much, much more," she had said seriously.

❧

This time, they competed in the first match, against the team from Queen Anne's County. Onstage, waiting for the competition to begin, Caitlin narrowed her eyes at the other team: three girls and a boy, all with serious, set expressions. Their captain had shoulder-length red hair and wore glasses.

"We can take them," Caitlin whispered to herself.

Beside her, Emma cast her an amused look. "Don't worry," she murmured. "You've got this."

And they began.

Caitlin felt like her hand had never moved so fast, slapping down on the buzzer almost as soon as a question was asked. And all four of them were snapping out the answers as if they had the internet installed in their brains.

"What is the title of the first book of C. S. Lewis's long fantasy series for children?"

Bzzz!

"*The Lion, the Witch and the Wardrobe.*"

"Which president later became chief justice of the Supreme Court?"

Bzzz!

"William Howard Taft."

"What is the rule that says an offensive player must not be closer to the other team's goal than either the ball or his second-to-last opponent?"

Bzzz!

"The offside rule in soccer. Which is also called football, in other countries."

"Where was the composer Frederic Chopin born?"

Bzzz!

"Frederick Chopin was from Poland."

"What mammal has the longest tongue in comparison to its body length?"

Bzzz!

"The tube-lipped nectar bat."

Natalia told Caitlin that last one very calmly but with a little smirk on her face.

"Way to go, Natalia," Caitlin murmured after she'd given the answer to the moderator.

"Shh!" said Natalia, the smirk growing more pronounced. "Listen for the next question."

The team from Queen Anne's County was pretty good, and they managed to answer some questions, but Caitlin's team won by a comfortable six points.

"We are on *fire*!" Caitlin whispered to the others as they filed down from the stage.

Of course, the problem with going first was that there were five more first-round matches to sit through before they would get to compete again.

They watched in polite silence for a while, Caitlin reminding herself that it was a good idea to get a sense of the other teams. After the second match, Natalia pulled out a notebook and started writing. "Give me a number," she whispered to Caitlin.

"Uh, three," Caitlin said. She went on observing the teams onstage. The team from Worcester County was definitely going to win, she thought. Their captain was a jockish-looking boy who was aggressive with the buzzer and almost always rang in first. She flexed her own fingers; she needed to keep them moving fast.

A few minutes later, the notebook landed on her lap. Across the top was written *MASH*.

"Again?" Caitlin whispered. "We already figured out my future."

Natalia shrugged. "Your future has changed. Look, you're going to live in San Francisco, in an apartment, and have no kids."

Mr. Patel was looking at them and frowning, so Caitlin lowered her voice even more. "Seems like a downgrade from a mansion in Hawaii."

"I just report what the fates tell me," Natalia whispered. "Good news, you'll be a doctor; bad news, you still end up married to Nathan."

Caitlin grimaced at her. "Nope. I'm not marrying any of the boys in our class. *If* I get married, it's going to be to someone I didn't know when they were at the nose-picking stage of life."

"It's okay," Natalia murmured. "I did mine, and I'm going to live in San Francisco, too. So, you can hide out at my place if Nathan still burps the alphabet when you're married." She nudged Caitlin. "I'm looking out for you, bestie."

On her other side, Caitlin could feel Emma shaking with silent laughter.

"You're ridiculous," Caitlin murmured. She couldn't stop smiling.

⁓

They broke for bag lunches before the second round.

"So, what do you think?" Emma asked, lifting the top slice of bread from her sandwich to take a peek at the filling. "Can we take them?"

Caitlin chewed and swallowed, thinking. "The team from Cecil County, definitely," she said. "They're not that fast with the buzzer; I think they mostly won because the other team wasn't prepared enough."

"The ones from Worcester were scary good, though," Natalia pointed out. "Did you see how fast their captain was?"

"The kids from the private school in Talbot County were pretty good, too," Zoe added. "And the other two teams were okay, but I think we might be better."

"We *will* be better," Caitlin said, determined.

They were playing against the team from the private school in Talbot County—Talbot Country Day—in the second round. Two girls with identical shoulder-length haircuts and two boys. One of the boys was the captain, sharp-faced with a very quick way of slapping at the buzzer.

Caitlin was still moving fast, too, but he was just as fast as she was. Maybe a little faster.

Bzzz!

"Talbot Country Day." The moderator called on the other team.

Caitlin stared down at her buzzer, feeling as if it had insulted her. She had been just a split second behind.

The skinny boy cleared his throat. "Benjamin Franklin was the first US ambassador to France."

I knew that. Caitlin clenched her teeth and resolved to move even faster.

Bzzz! She was first that time. And she knew who had written *The Secret Garden.*

"Frances Hodgson Burnett."

Bzzz!

"The word for no score in tennis is love."

Bzzz!

"Seismometers are used to measure earthquakes."

Bzzz!

"Gauguin shared a house with Van Gogh in Arles, France."

They were evenly matched, trading off answers as if they were taking turns on purpose. At the end of the twenty questions, the teams were tied. Caitlin wiped her forehead: She was actually sweating from tension and from lunging for the buzzer.

"Good work, Talbot Country Day and Waverly Middle School," the moderator chirped. "Now we're going to move into the sudden death round. The first team to answer a question correctly will win the match."

Caitlin tensed, her hand poised directly above the buzzer as she waited for the question. On the other side of the stage, she could see the Talbot Country Day captain's hand hovering above his own buzzer. It was going to come down to speed, she was sure of it.

"What US state has the oldest capitol building still in use?" the moderator read.

A thrill shot through Caitlin, her hand in motion almost before the moderator had stopped speaking.

Bzzz!

She shared one quick look of triumph with her teammates before saying—for the win—"Maryland."

～⁓～

Their families and Mr. Patel took the team out for dinner in Annapolis. They chose a crab house by the water and sat out on the deck, the warm spring breeze lifting their hair and sending napkins to the ground. Newspaper covered the tables, and the cheerful waitress brought out buckets of red steamed crabs and pitchers of soda and iced tea, and nutcrackers for everyone to crack the crabs' claws and pull out the sweet meat. In a few minutes, everybody's hands were coated with Old Bay Seasoning, spicy and sticky.

Caitlin looked around the table at the others, feeling a warm surge of affection: her parents, deep in conversation with Emma's parents; Mateo and Tomás clicking crab claws at each other; her own brother, Robbie, talking over his college plans with the twins' dad, who taught him at the high school; even Mr. Patel looking less like a teacher and more relaxed and just like a friend of their families who had come along for the meal.

And her friends—her *best* friends. Natalia, waving her hands as she talked, already had a piece of crab shell caught in her hair. Zoe, who was usually so laid-back, was practically bouncing in her seat as she described to her grandmother how she'd felt when they got the last question. And Emma, who had never been to a crab house before, wiping her hands between every bite and gradually destroying a whole pile of napkins. They were her friends, and her team, and they had *won*.

Caitlin knew that the friendship part was more important than the winning part. She wasn't going to get carried away again. But winning felt *awesome*. "Hey," she said to everyone at the table. "I want to make a toast."

"A toast!" Everyone smiled and quieted, turned toward her.

"I just wanted to thank my team. Natalia, Emma, and Zoe have worked really hard. They're so smart, and they've kept me from getting too crazy. I'm really happy we're on this team together, and that we're friends. There's nobody I'd rather learn random facts with." She raised her glass. "Thanks, you guys."

All around the table, her friends and family raised their glasses to toast, and Natalia leaned forward, clinking her glass against Caitlin's. "Thank *you*, Caitlin," she said. "I know we get frustrated with each other, but you are an *awesome* captain."

⁓

Monday morning, Mr. Patel asked Caitlin to stay back after class. "You girls have done amazingly well," he told her, rummaging through the stacks of paper on his desk. "This is the first time our trivia team has made it as far as the state level. I'm so proud of all of you."

"Thanks, Mr. Patel," Caitlin said. "I hope we make it even further."

He grinned at her. "Well, I hope so, too, but you should be very proud of yourselves in any case." He found what he was looking for on his desk—a large manila envelope—and held it out to her. "I just got the official packet of information for the team about the state competition. Rules and location and stuff like that. As the team captain, can I count on you to share it with the other girls?"

"Absolutely." Caitlin took the envelope just as the bell rang for the start of the next period and hurried out to her next class.

She sat through science impatiently, eager to see what was in the envelope, and got to their lunch table first. Peeling open the flap of the envelope, Caitlin pulled out a thick stack of paper and flipped through. There were directions to the hall in Baltimore where the competition was being held, a list of nearby restaurants, information about prizes, a review of the rules, a study guide, permission slips for their parents to sign. Everything looked pretty reasonable.

She turned over a page and hesitated, confused. This was the first page of another, separate packet, its staple caught on the staple on her packet. And on the top, it read *Maryland State Middle School Trivia Championship: Judges' Packet.*

This can't be right. Frowning, Caitlin turned through the pages, reading more closely. Some of the information was the same as in the student packet: directions, restaurants, rules, prizes. There were also instructions about *how* to ask the questions, and Caitlin grinned in recognition when she read what the moderators were supposed to do: use the school's name when addressing the captains, keep a strict eye on the time, speak slowly. She turned another page and froze.

Contest Questions, the page read. *Answer sheet will be supplied on the day of the competition*, and below: *Where did Francis Scott Key write "The Star-Spangled Banner"? What is the only marsupial native to the United States? What is the youngest age at which Olympic gymnasts can compete?* It went on for pages and pages, question after question.

What *was* this? Caitlin turned the pages slowly, reading the questions.

Was it some kind of study guide? They'd *given* it to her. They wouldn't have given her the real questions. Would they? She flipped back to the first page. It *said* Judges' Packet.

How could this have happened?

Caitlin's mouth went dry, and she realized her heart was pounding hard. She'd accidentally gotten the questions for the state trivia competition. What was she supposed to do now?

Chapter Seven

"Hey, Caitlin."

Without consciously thinking about it, Caitlin slipped the packet of papers under her books before she turned around. "Hey, guys," she said as the twins sat down. "Where's Emma?"

"She stopped to talk to Ms. Brandon about summer training," Zoe said. Ms. Brandon, the gym teacher, also coached Emma's soccer team in the fall.

Should I tell them about the judges' packet? Caitlin wondered. She decided against it for now: She needed some time to understand what had happened. Had the people in charge just accidentally sent her the questions that would be in the state finals? She couldn't help glancing at the edge of the packet, peeking out from beneath her books. *Is finding this a good thing or a bad thing?* She didn't know how to feel.

"We're only practicing for twenty-five minutes, right?" Natalia asked warily. "And then we're relaxing for the rest of lunch? I can go talk to my other friends?"

"Of course," Caitlin said. "We agreed. But Emma had better hurry up, or we won't get to practice." She brushed her thumb over the edge of the packet. *Should I tell them?* she wondered again.

"I think this counts as relaxation time, though," Zoe said. "Oh, hi, Emma."

Emma dropped her little lunch cooler in the center of the table and took a seat. "I am *so* going to improve my skills over the summer," she told them. "Ms. Brandon is running a soccer intensive in the park."

"You know that we don't have any idea what that means," Zoe said, reaching for the cooler.

Emma slapped her hand away. "It means I'm going to be *awesome.*"

"You're already awesome," Natalia said loyally. "What did Uncle Brian send for lunch?"

Emma unzipped the cooler. "Prosciutto-and-fig-spread sandwiches on Italian bread," she said, handing them out. "Plus black bean, quinoa, and citrus salads on the side."

Caitlin looked at her sandwich with alarm. The meat in it was cut really thin and was a pale pink with whitish streaks, and the spread was dark brown and thick, with pieces of something—fig, she guessed—in it. "Do I like prosciutto?" she asked. "What *is* prosciutto exactly?" She thought for a second. "Do I like figs?" Caitlin's parents cooked a lot for her family, but they were much more likely to just roast a chicken or make a salad than to experiment the way Emma's dad did.

"Prosciutto's Italian ham," Emma told her. "It's delicious—try it."

Apprehensively, Caitlin bit into the sandwich. The bread was chewy, and the meat and spread together were salty and sweet at the same time. "It's good!" she said, a little surprised, and Emma smiled at her.

"More importantly," Natalia said around a bite of her own sandwich, "what's for dessert?"

"Dad went on a macaron baking binge yesterday," Emma told them, grinning. "The whole kitchen was covered with almond flour. I brought raspberry and chocolate ones, and there's lemon back at the house."

"Oh my gosh," Zoe said. She held out a hand and wiggled her fingers demandingly. "Hand some over right now, I'm going to eat them with my lunch instead of for dessert."

When everyone had a couple of the pink and brown sandwich cookies, they turned expectantly to Caitlin.

"Ready to start practice?" Emma asked.

"Yeah," Caitlin said. She glanced again at the pile of books concealing the packet that Mr. Patel had given her and thought for a second about grabbing the pages of questions. Instead, she opened her binder and pulled out the flash cards. "I thought this week could be about everything every day, instead of one category each day," she told the others. "That's the way the actual competitions go, so maybe we should practice going straight from art to sports and then history or whatever instead of doing all the same subjects together."

"Sounds good," Natalia said, and the others nodded.

Caitlin picked up the top card, a green animals-and-nature card, and stared at it. It read: *How old is a male peacock when it starts to grow its showy train of feathers?* Answer: *About three years old.*

She opened her mouth to ask the question, and then thought of the pile of papers beneath her books, and of the questions she *knew* would be part of the competition. Why would she want to waste time studying something that wasn't on that list? Instead of asking the question in front of her, she cleared her throat and asked: "What is the only marsupial native to the United States?"

"The Virginia opossum," Natalia said immediately. "Usually called the opossum. Or just possum."

"Correct," Caitlin said. She wasn't completely sure— there hadn't been any answers on the list of questions she'd found—but it sounded right. *I have all the questions we should study,* she thought, feeling a little dizzy. *We could practice every single question that's in the competition.* "Hey," she went on, "we're practicing this afternoon, too, right? At your house?" she asked the twins. Now that the finals were so close, the girls had decided to meet more often.

"Just for an hour," Zoe said. "Natalia's got a bunch of dogs to walk. But we promise to be super-focused."

"Good," said Caitlin. "I've got something I need to talk to you guys about."

~⌒~

Today, Caitlin welcomed the noise and confusion of the after-school Martinez household. Mateo and Tomás were running around and around the kitchen table, their sneakered feet thudding and squeaking, and the vacuum cleaner roared from the living room, where Natalia and Zoe's dad was already home from the high school and tidying up. With all the noise, it was less obvious that Caitlin herself was being unusually quiet.

All day at school, she'd been distracted, sneaking peeks at the judges' packet and its questions.

What is the largest city in terms of square miles in the United States?

Where does the Venus flytrap grow in the wild?

Who was the longest-lived former president?

What is Bloomsday?

So many questions! Some of them she knew the answers to already, through all the studying they'd done, but a lot of them she didn't. Even though the answers weren't included in the packet, having these questions to look up would really help their studying.

Would that be an okay thing to do? It wasn't like anyone would be *giving* them the answers; they'd still have to figure those out on their own. It would take *hours* to look up the answers to all those questions, and then they'd still have to study them hard if they wanted to know them for the competition. The packet would be more like a study guide than anything else.

But if anyone found out she had the questions, would she get in trouble? She hadn't asked for the wrong packet; she hadn't gotten it on purpose. It wasn't her fault.

She'd thought about keeping the judges' packet secret from her teammates. What if she just added the questions to their study cards? No one else would know. Then the other girls wouldn't have to worry about it the way she was; they would just be studying the right answers. It really *would* be a study packet then.

She stared down at the table, thinking. Would that be the best thing to do? But that didn't feel right. It would be like she was lying to them—to her team.

"Okay," Natalia said, grabbing a bag of chips from the counter and gently disentangling herself from Tomás, who was hanging on to her shoulders now and pretending to be a monkey. "On to our room, study pals."

Caitlin and Emma followed the twins up to their shared room. "I did some more review of earthquakes and volcanoes and other natural disasters last night," Natalia told them as she flopped onto her unmade bed. "So, I'm extra ready for this study session. Go ahead and ask me a question about landslides. I am a disaster expert."

"Which explains why your side of the room is such a disaster area." Zoe grabbed a handful of chips out of the bag and plopped down on her own neatly made bed on the other side of the room. "Should we start with a nature question, then?"

Caitlin claimed Natalia's desk chair and waited as Emma settled herself on the floor, her back against Natalia's bed, and took her own handful of chips. Once everyone was sitting down, Caitlin drew in a deep breath.

"Listen, I need to show you guys something," she said. She dug in her bag, pulled out the packet of papers Mr. Patel had given her, and handed them to Emma. Natalia leaned over Emma's shoulder to read, and Zoe crossed the room to sit beside her so that she could see, too.

"Oh," Emma said. "The info for the state championship. Cool."

She turned a page and Natalia reached out and pointed at something. "We should get our parents to take us *there* for dinner after the competition. I love Thai food."

"Baltimore has some good restaurants," Zoe said. "I could go for some pad thai right now."

"No, go farther on in the packet," Caitlin told them. She watched, her stomach twisting with nervousness, as Emma turned over page after page until she came to the end of the student packet.

Caitlin could tell when they reached the next packet, because all three girls frowned, confused. Zoe raised an eyebrow questioningly. "How did you get a judges' packet?" she asked. She reached over Emma's shoulder and turned a page. "This has the *final questions* on it, Caitlin."

Caitlin shrugged and spread out her hands in a "who knows?" gesture. "It was attached to my packet. The staples were stuck together. It must have been an accident."

Natalia grinned and sat up straight on her bed. "But this is great!" she said. "They just gave us the questions that are going to be in the competition."

"You think we should use them?" Zoe said skeptically. "Isn't that cheating?"

"It's not like we tried to get them," Natalia said. "They *gave* them to us. And it's not answers, only the questions. We'd still have to do all the work of looking things up. It's like a study guide."

"That's exactly what *I* thought," Caitlin told her. Hearing Natalia said this made her feel more confident about it. She knew Natalia was a good person:

She wouldn't actually cheat. "It's just helping us; it's not giving us the answers." They grinned at each other.

"Wait a second," Emma said. She stared at Caitlin. "*You* think we should use the questions, too?"

"Well . . ." Caitlin hesitated. "I mean, they'd give us a real advantage. And Natalia's right—it's not like we stole them or asked for them or anything. If we find out what the questions are through sheer luck, why shouldn't we use them?"

"Because we'd be *cheating*!" Emma told her. "Caitlin, I can't believe you think this is a good idea." She shook her head, her lips pressed tightly together, and said, "We should take the packet to Mr. Patel and tell him what happened."

"I don't think it *is* cheating," Caitlin said stubbornly. "It's only a guide to some questions we *might* be asked. How is that different from a study guide?"

Emma folded her arms. "Because it came directly from the test officials. We have to tell Mr. Patel."

Zoe and Caitlin exchanged a look. Zoe was frowning now, and in her dark eyes Caitlin could read her own worries about what would happen if anyone knew they had the judges' packet.

"If we do that, we might get into trouble," Zoe said slowly. "Mr. Patel will know we looked at the questions. We might get kicked out of the competition."

"We won't get in trouble if we go to him right away," Emma argued.

"I don't want to," Caitlin said. "I've seen the questions now; he'd make me drop out of the contest. Zoe's right—he might make the whole team drop out. And I can't go to him right away anyway. Not anymore. I've had it all day. I've been reading it."

"It's the right thing to do, though. No matter what happens," Emma insisted, looking back and forth between Caitlin and the twins.

Caitlin bit her lip. Knowing the questions was such a clear path to winning. And they'd still be doing a lot of the work themselves. A little spark of anger lit in Caitlin's chest. Emma had been with her every step of the way: studying, organizing everybody, being the best of her teammates. Why was she turning against her now? Didn't she want to win just as much as Caitlin did?

"I think we should use them as a study guide, like Natalia said. We'll still be doing all the work," Caitlin argued, getting to her feet.

"Yes!" Natalia said, jumping up and coming to stand with Caitlin. "I totally agree."

Caitlin felt a warm glow in her chest. She and Natalia were thinking the same way, best friends like they always were. Maybe they had different study styles, but they usually agreed on the things that mattered.

Emma turned to Zoe, her face creased in a worried frown. "You don't agree with them, do you?"

Zoe hesitated, and then said slowly, "It's a little bit shady using the questions, I know, but they *did* give them to us. We didn't go looking for them. And what Caitlin says is true: We'll still be doing a lot of the work. I think I want to go with the majority rule here."

Emma inhaled sharply and glared at them, her cheeks bright pink. Instead of worried, she looked furious. "I can't believe you guys," she said, almost spitting out the words. "You should be *ashamed*. Is that really the way you want to win?"

Caitlin was used to gentle, soft-spoken Emma; she'd never seen her so angry. They were all on their feet now, the twins on either side of Caitlin, a united front against Emma. "Are you going to tell on us?" Caitlin asked, glaring at her. Would Emma really turn them in?

Faced with her friends standing like a wall against her, Emma's shoulders slumped, and she looked down at the floor. There was a long pause. "No," she said finally, sounding defeated. "I'm not going to tell on you guys to Mr. Patel. But I don't want to be part of this. If you guys are going to cheat, then I quit the team."

Without looking at them or even raising her eyes from the floor, she brushed past Caitlin and crossed the room to the door. None of them said anything, but Caitlin's chest felt hollow with panic. Was Emma really going to just leave?

Emma walked out the door and closed it quietly behind her.

The room felt so full of silence that Caitlin couldn't manage to break it, couldn't say anything at all.

Chapter Eight

The next morning, their special cafeteria study table felt oddly empty without Emma. She was on the other side of the room, sitting at their old table with their other friends instead. Caitlin watched as Emma turned to talk to Heather from her swim team.

"I wonder what they're saying," Caitlin said to Natalia. "You don't think she told anyone else about the judges' packet, do you?"

Natalia shook her head. "Emma promised she wasn't going to tell on us. And she wouldn't gossip about us to other kids."

"I guess you're right," Caitlin said, feeling comforted. Emma was trustworthy. *Of course that's the problem.* She frowned at the thought. There wasn't anything *untrust-*worthy about what they were doing, was there?

Zoe came over, carrying a blue bag, and sat down. "Emma gave me our lunches," she told them. She had an odd smile on her face, as if she was trying not to seem upset. "We're having chicken salad wraps with Havarti cheese, sesame sticks on the side, and white chocolate–cranberry cookies."

Caitlin reached out and took one of the wraps. It looked good and smelled good, but she didn't have any appetite for it. She bit in, and it didn't taste as good as their lunches from Emma's dad usually did. She chewed and swallowed the one bite, and then stopped. Maybe she just wasn't hungry. Natalia and Zoe were eating slowly. Maybe they didn't feel hungry, either.

"I guess we need to find another person for the team," Caitlin said glumly. "We have to have four people to compete."

Zoe sighed. "Maybe Mr. Patel can recommend somebody."

Natalia put down her wrap. "Would we tell the new person?" she asked. "About the packet?"

Caitlin stared down at the table. "Maybe not," she said slowly. "They might not understand." Her stomach was starting to hurt. If they weren't cheating, why didn't she want anyone else to know?

From the other table, Emma looked over, and their eyes met for a moment. Then Emma looked away. Her mouth was a tight, unhappy line.

Something wet hit Caitlin's fingers, and she realized she was squeezing her wrap so hard, the dressing was oozing out. She put it down and wiped her fingers on her napkin.

"Let's get started," she said. "I stayed up last night researching the answers to a bunch of the questions and added them to our card deck. And I took out the cards we know aren't included." She dug into her bag and pulled out the stack of multicolored index cards, now much thinner and consisting only of the questions from the packet. "It's the same color scheme still. Green for nature and everything."

"It's a lot less to study now," Zoe said. Her voice sounded falsely upbeat, as if she was trying to sound enthusiastic, and failing.

Caitlin plucked an American history card from the

stack first. "Okay, either one of you can answer. What name was the town of Atlanta, Georgia, founded under?"

Zoe and Natalia looked at each other. Natalia shrugged.

"Trick question," Zoe said eventually. "Atlanta, Georgia, was founded as Atlanta, Georgia."

"Nope," Caitlin said, and read off the card, "Atlanta, Georgia, was founded in 1837 as Terminus, Georgia, because a train line terminated there."

"I had no idea," Zoe said. She reached for the cards. "Let me ask one."

As Zoe looked through the flash cards, Caitlin found her eyes drawn again toward the lunch table where Emma and their other friends were sitting. Emma was quiet, listening to Vivian and Heather and some of the other girls. She was frowning a little. *She looks sort of sad*, Caitlin thought, wondering if Emma was missing sitting at their study table, if she wished she was prepping for the competition, too.

"Caitlin!" Zoe called her name sharply, as if she had said it a couple times before.

"What?" Almost guiltily, Caitlin jerked her gaze away from the other table.

"I asked you which US state doesn't have any native species of venomous snakes."

"Uh." Caitlin stared up at the ceiling, trying to remember. She had written this down, just yesterday. Her mind was blank. "Um. It would have to be somewhere cold. Michigan?"

"You were right about the cold, but actually it's Alaska." Zoe slid the cards toward Natalia, but now Natalia was looking over toward the other table, her face wistful. Zoe looked down at the table, her shoulders drooping. Across at the other table, Emma was twisting her hands in her lap anxiously.

We're all sad, Caitlin thought. *This doesn't feel right without Emma.*

If Emma wasn't happy, either, maybe Caitlin would be able to convince her to come back to the team.

No. She dismissed the idea. *Emma doesn't want to cheat. She won't come back.*

But we're not cheating.

Are we?

That night, Caitlin couldn't sleep. She shifted and rolled from one side to the other, trying to get comfortable, and kept opening her eyes to check the time on the digital clock on her bedside table. *10:40*, it read. *11:20*. *11:55*.

Finally, she rolled over onto her back and stared up at the glowing stars on her ceiling. Natalia had helped her put those up when they were nine after Caitlin bought them on a class trip to the science museum. Looking back, it seemed like things had been a lot easier then.

There was a funny hollowness in the bottom of Caitlin's stomach, an anxious, tense sensation. She had the terrible feeling that she always got if it got late enough and she still couldn't sleep, where all the most embarrassing things that had ever happened to her flooded through her mind and she began worrying about things that she couldn't do anything about.

In the middle of remembering the time she had fallen off the monkey bars in fourth grade and everyone had seen her underwear, Caitlin couldn't stand it anymore.

Sitting up, she fumbled around with the dark shapes on her bedside table until she found her phone. Leaning

back on her pillow, she texted Natalia: *Are you awake?*
I can't sleep.

A few minutes later, the phone beeped. *Me, neither,*
Natalia had written.

Caitlin hesitated, and then typed: *Do you think that*
Emma's still mad at us?

There was a long pause, long enough that Caitlin
wondered if Natalia had fallen asleep, or if Natalia's
mom had caught her texting this late at night and taken
her phone away.

Finally, Natalia texted back: *I don't think she's mad at*
us exactly. She and Aunt Amy came over after dinner to work
on some centerpieces for the B and B dining room tables and
she seemed normal. A little quiet maybe.

Caitlin sighed. *That* was the problem when your best
friends were all related to each other. They couldn't
get *too* mad at each other, not for long, because they
had known each other since they were babies digging
in the sand on the beach together. And in the backs of
their minds, they knew that, no matter what happened
in sixth grade, they'd still spend family vacations and

holidays together, until way, way in the future, when they'd be old ladies rocking side by side on the front porch.

Natalia, Zoe, and Emma couldn't stop knowing each other, no matter what happened or how angry they got, but any of them could stop being friends with Caitlin, if they wanted to. An uncomfortable pang of anxiety wiggled through her.

Did she seem like she was mad at ME? Caitlin typed, her face growing hot.

This time Natalia wrote back fast. *She didn't seem like she was mad at anybody anymore. Just kind of sad, maybe.*

Caitlin sighed and rubbed her forehead. She didn't want Emma to be *sad*, either. *I wish she was still on the team*, she wrote. *It's not the same without her.*

I do, too, Natalia wrote. *I wish she would try and see things our way. She's really stubborn when she thinks she's right.*

Caitlin bit her lip. The uncomfortable feeling inside her was getting worse. They really were just using the judges' packet like a study guide; they were still doing the work of figuring out the answers and studying themselves. But was it fair that they got a guide to what the questions were going to be when none of the other teams did?

She'd made Emma promise that she wasn't going to turn them in to Mr. Patel. And she'd been relieved when the twins had reassured her that Emma wouldn't tell anyone else. Caitlin pulled her legs close to her chest and rested her chin on her knees. If she was so sure that what they were doing was okay, she wondered, why was she also so scared of anybody finding out about it?

She began texting again. *Are you sure that Emma's not actually right? Because I feel like she might be. We might have made a mistake.*

There was a long pause. Then Natalia wrote back, *I think so, too.*

Caitlin thought for a moment, and then typed, *Would you be mad if maybe we didn't use the questions we found to study with? Would Zoe?*

I'd be okay with it, Natalia wrote back immediately. *And I think Zoe would, too. I miss Emma. It was more fun with all four of us on the team, even though we didn't know what the questions were going to be.* There was another, shorter pause, and then she added, *But we DO know the questions. We can't just forget them. What should we do?*

Caitlin sighed. She felt less miserable now than she had all day; the weird uncomfortable feeling inside her was gone. But there was a new nervous prickling on the back of her neck. What *were* they going to do? They had seen the questions, and it didn't really matter if they didn't use them to study from now on. Caitlin was right: They weren't going to be able forget them all, even if they tried.

I think we should all talk about it, she wrote. *Emma, too. We're going to have to make the decision as a team.*

Okay, Natalia texted back. *We'll figure it out!*

Caitlin's eyelids were suddenly heavy with tiredness. *I better go to sleep,* Caitlin texted to Natalia. *Good night.*

Natalia sent a sleepy emoji, a string of *zzz*'s coming from its mouth. *Good night.*

Chapter Nine

"Are you sure you're supposed to go over *this* early?" Caitlin's brother, Robbie, asked, squinting in the early morning sunshine as he pulled up outside Seaview House. The sun had just risen, and the sky was bright with pink and gold.

"I told you, we're all going to have breakfast together," Caitlin said, looking up at the bed-and-breakfast. It had a not-quite-awake yet look to it: A lot of the window shades were drawn, and the porch light was still burning from the night before, its light looking thin and artificial in the sunlight. Since she and Natalia had made up their minds that the *whole* team—including Emma—needed to talk, Caitlin wanted to do it as soon as possible. She'd texted Emma and the twins right after she got up, and Emma had invited them all over for breakfast.

"You good?" Robbie asked, looking past her at Seaview House. "You're going to ride the school bus with Emma, right?" Robbie ran on the track at the high school every morning before class; he'd offered to drop Caitlin off for breakfast and a "study session" on his way.

"That's the plan," Caitlin said cheerfully. "Thanks for the ride." She climbed out of the car and watched as Robbie drove away. Then she turned and climbed the steps to the front porch of Seaview House.

Once she was in front of the door, she suddenly felt chilly. Crossing her arms and shivering, she looked up toward the top floor, where Emma and her family lived. What if Emma was really mad at her? She had invited them all over for breakfast, but that didn't mean she wasn't angry.

If she's mad, she's mad, Caitlin decided. *But I won't know if I don't find out.* Uncrossing her arms, she tapped lightly on the door. Emma had warned her not to ring the bell, to avoid waking the B and B guests.

The door swung open almost immediately, as if Emma had been waiting for her knock. Emma hesitated in the doorway, looking as if she didn't quite know what to do—almost as if she was slightly afraid of what Caitlin might say.

Caitlin felt terrible seeing Emma so pale and nervous. Her friend was *sad* because of something she, Caitlin, had done. Caitlin took a small step forward, and then a step back. "Hi," she said.

Emma pushed her hair back behind her ears, nervously. "Come on in," she said.

The front rooms and the dining room of the B and B were quiet and dim, but the kitchen was bright and full of delicious smells of frying and baking. Emma's dad was standing by the stove, frying fat sausages in a pan.

"Good morning, Caitlin," he said cheerfully. "What do you feel like for breakfast?"

Caitlin felt shy at the question. The bed-and-breakfast was *kind* of like a restaurant—at least at breakfast time—but she wasn't a B and B guest, so she couldn't just order whatever she wanted, could she?

"I guess whatever you're making," she said. "I like most things."

Emma opened the refrigerator and handed her father a carton of eggs. "I'm going to have a croissant and scrambled eggs with some fruit."

"Oh, that sounds good," Caitlin said. "Wow, I usually just have cereal or toaster waffles."

"One of the benefits of living in a bed-and-breakfast," Emma's dad told her. "On the downside, Emma has to be quiet in the morning so she doesn't bother the guests, but on the upside, there's always a wide selection of breakfast food."

They heard the front door open and shut, and a minute later, Zoe came into the kitchen. "Morning," she said. Her hair was ruffled as if she'd just rolled out of bed, and she was moving more slowly than usual. Zoe was *not* a morning person.

"Hey, Zoe," Caitlin said. "Where's Natalia?"

"Um," Zoe said, plopping down on a stool at the counter. "Dogs. She has a German shepherd and a Maltese to walk before breakfast." Zoe closed her eyes and rested her head on the counter.

"Orange juice or pineapple?" Emma asked Caitlin.

"Pineapple, please."

Emma poured herself and Caitlin glasses of pineapple juice and slid a glass of orange juice to Zoe, who propped her head up on her hand and took a few sips.

"The guests are having breakfast in their rooms," Emma's dad said, "so you girls get the dining room all to yourselves." He folded an omelet over and added it to one of the plates beside him, and then loaded up a couple trays and left the kitchen.

Zoe seemed to be awake enough to actually get herself some food now, and she headed for the stove and started to fill two plates with sausages, croissants, and fruit. "I'll get stuff for Natalia," she offered. "I know what she wants."

Caitlin and Emma picked out their own food and followed Zoe out to the dining room. The sun had risen higher and was shining through the windows, making the dining room, with its pastel-painted tables and fresh flowers, sunny and inviting.

The front door banged as Natalia came in, leading two dogs. "Hey," she said, and disappeared up the stairs, the dogs padding after her. A moment later, she came back down and joined them at the table. The twins started eating, but Caitlin, still awkwardly standing, looked at Emma and found Emma looking back at her, biting her lip.

"I'm sorry," said Caitlin, pulling Emma into a quick hug.

"I'm sorry, too," Emma said, wiping her eyes as they let go of each other. "I didn't mean to yell at you guys. And I felt bad about not sitting with you in the cafeteria, but I just couldn't when you were all practicing and I wasn't on the team anymore."

"We missed you, too," Caitlin said, feeling on the verge of tears herself. "It wasn't fair of me to put you in a spot where you felt like you had to quit the team." She hesitated, hating having to admit that she had been wrong. "I think you were right," she confessed at last. "I should have told Mr. Patel about the packet as soon as I found it." She looked around at the others. "Even though I thought it was basically just a study guide, I felt *horrible* using it. I felt like a criminal."

"I felt the same way," Zoe said. "I didn't think it was a

big deal at first, but then it just felt wrong." Her sister nodded in agreement.

"I think Emma was right that using the questions was cheating, even though we were looking up the answers ourselves," Caitlin went on. Her voice sounded small and quiet to her own ears. She stared down at her plate. "I'm going to talk to Mr. Patel today. I'll tell him what happened and that I studied the questions." She swallowed. She *hated* getting in trouble. "I'll tell him that I was the one who did it." She looked up to meet her friends' gazes. "I mean, I gave you guys the questions," she said.

Natalia rolled her eyes. "Don't get crazy, Caitlin," she said. "Of course we're not going to let you tell him it was all your fault. We chose to use the questions, too, so we're just as much to blame."

"Except for Emma," Zoe pointed out. "She told us not to."

Emma jutted out her chin stubbornly. "I'm not ditching you guys to take all the blame," she told them. "After all, I didn't report it, even though I knew it was wrong. We should all turn ourselves in together."

Even the idea of Mr. Patel being mad at and disappointed in them wasn't quite so terrible, if her friends were going to stand by her. Caitlin smiled a little. "Thanks, guys."

"So, that's settled," Natalia said. "Do we have time for some of Uncle Brian's special hot chocolate before the school bus?"

Emma looked up at the clock. "If we hurry," she said. "I know how to make it. The secret ingredients are vanilla and cinnamon. And really high-quality chocolate."

Caitlin swallowed. The thought of confessing to Mr. Patel made her mouth dry and sour with anxiety, but something sweet would certainly help.

Chapter Ten

"Okay," said Caitlin to the others. "We're going to do this." She took a deep breath and stared at the closed door to the social studies classroom. "Okay." She still couldn't bring herself to face Mr. Patel.

"Sheesh, Caitlin, *okay*, okay," Zoe said, exasperated. "Here, let me." She reached past Caitlin, tapped on the door, and pushed it open.

Mr. Patel, seated at his desk, looked up from the papers he was correcting. "It's my champion trivia team!" he said cheerfully. "Shouldn't you girls be in homeroom?"

"No. I mean, yes," Caitlin corrected herself. "But we need to talk to you."

"Okay." Mr. Patel pushed back from his desk and gave

them his full attention. "Sock it to me, kids. Do you need help getting ready for the state competition?"

"Not exactly," Caitlin said. She fished the judges' packet out of her backpack and slowly put it down on the desk in front of Mr. Patel. She stepped back, feeling slightly sick.

"What's this?" Mr. Patel adjusted his glasses, picked up the packet, and flipped through it. As he read, his eyebrows steadily rose.

When he'd finished, he placed the papers back on his desk, pushed his glasses up his nose, and stared at them. "Where did you get this?"

Caitlin bowed her head and looked down at her feet. "It was in the envelope with the packet for contestants. I found it—the staples were caught together. I think it must have gotten stuck into our packet by mistake." She scraped the toe of her shoe along the floor, not wanting to look up at Mr. Patel as she confessed. "We researched the answers to the questions and started studying them, but then we realized that it really *was* cheating, even though it didn't feel like it at first. We're sorry."

"Not Emma, though," Natalia added from beside Caitlin. "She didn't want to use the questions from the judges' packet at all and she didn't practice with us when we used those questions."

Emma crossed her arms defiantly. "I knew exactly what was going on, so I'm just as much to blame as the others," she said.

"Well, that's debatable," Zoe said. "But anyway, Mr. Patel, the rest of us should have known better, too."

"I'm the captain, and I found the questions and decided to share them with the others," Caitlin insisted. "I'm the one responsible."

"We all did it," Natalia argued. "Except Emma, but she wants to take the blame anyway. We *are* sorry, though."

Mr. Patel sighed and clasped his hands together on his desk. "I'm sorry, too," he said at last. "I should have looked through the packet before I passed it on to Caitlin. By not being thorough, I put you all in a difficult position."

"Oh." Caitlin exchanged surprised glances with the other girls. She hadn't thought of it that way. "But we should have told you right away. And we shouldn't have started studying the questions from it."

"That's true." Mr. Patel looked at her seriously. "I do appreciate your honesty in coming to me about this now. It would have been easy for you girls to hide this from everyone and to cheat, but you knew that it would be wrong. I'm glad you came to me. But I'll have to contact the organizers of the contest. And I can't imagine you'll be allowed to compete, as you've seen the questions that will be asked."

Caitlin's heart sank. She had known that this would happen—how *could* they possibly be in the competition, when they had such a big advantage over everyone else?—but a part of her had been hoping that somehow it would work out. It hurt to hear Mr. Patel actually say they wouldn't be allowed in the state competition.

She looked at her teammates. Natalia was sticking her chin out like she was trying not to cry. Zoe was staring at her shoes. Emma met Caitlin's eyes and gave her a sad, small smile.

Caitlin turned back to Mr. Patel and looked him in the eye. "We understand."

❧

The next day in homeroom, the four girls were quiet. "I think this should be the summer that we all become extraordinary," Natalia said, clearly attempting to break the silence.

"Aren't we already extraordinary?" Caitlin said, pulling pencils out of her pencil case and lining them up on her desk in perfect parallel. "My mother has told me *I* am extraordinary, anyway."

"Oh, ha ha," Natalia said. "I mean that this summer we should pick a couple things that we want to get really good at and spend our time practicing them. By the time we start seventh grade, we'll be masters of our chosen fields. By high school, we'd be practically professionals."

"Okay, I'll bite," Zoe said, turning around from her desk in front of Caitlin. "What are our chosen fields in this plan of yours?"

"Well," Natalia said thoughtfully. "We could learn to sail. Or to make cannoli. Or, I don't know, build an amazing tree house and perfect our design and architecture skills." She grinned and spread her arms wide. "I would make an amazing architect. I could build the city of the future. Nataliaopolis."

Caitlin knew that Natalia was trying to cheer them all up. Maybe they weren't going to get to compete in the state finals in Baltimore, or to move on to the nationals in glamorous New York City, but they'd done really well and could be proud of themselves.

"I'm sorry we're not going to get to New York," Caitlin told her friends. "It would have been fun to see the places we wrote about, Emma."

She imagined Athena from their story, calling a hawk from Central Park to her, making vines grow through the middle of the ice rink in Rockefeller Center. *We'll get to New York City sometime, though*, she thought wistfully.

Emma sat up straighter, looking startled. "I forgot to tell you!" she said. "I submitted our story to the literary magazine. I turned it in the day you showed us the packet, and then I forgot all about it after we argued."

"Oh." Caitlin blinked. "Wow. Are you sure it was ready?" The story had been so much fun to write, and *she* had thought it was really good. But that wasn't the same as being sure she wanted other people to read it.

"Yeah," said Emma. She grinned at Caitlin reassuringly. "That was always the plan, right? And we were finished."

"I guess," Caitlin said, feeling a little sick at the idea of all the eighth graders on the literary magazine staff reading their story.

"*And,*" Emma went on, dragging out the word teasingly, "I got a text this morning from the editor. Our story's going to be published in the literary magazine! They really liked it!"

"Really?" Caitlin said, stunned. The eighth graders had liked their story! Caitlin felt herself begin to smile. The heavy feeling of dread at having to explain themselves to Mr. Patel hadn't gone away. But the story *was* good, she was sure of it. And now it was going to be in the magazine. At least they had *something* to look forward to.

The bell rang, and their homeroom teacher, Mr. Thomas, came to the front of the room. "Quiet down, kids," he said, rapping his fist on the edge of the whiteboard to get the class's attention. "I have a few announcements to make."

Emma and Zoe turned back around to give Mr. Thomas their attention, but Natalia only shifted closer to Caitlin and dropped her voice to a whisper. "You know," she murmured, "I really do think your and Emma's story is awesome. The literary magazine is lucky to be able to publish it."

"Thanks," Caitlin whispered back. Her cheeks felt a little warm at the praise, but it was a good kind of warm.

Natalia's voice got even quieter, as if she really didn't want anyone but Caitlin to hear what she was saying, and she stared down at her desk. "I was kind of jealous at first that you guys were spending so much time together and doing something without me," she whispered.

Caitlin glanced at her quickly. Natalia's cheeks were flushed, as if she were a little embarrassed. "Really? You were jealous?" she asked. After feeling just slightly on the outside of the other girls' tight family group, it was weird—and weirdly comforting—to hear that Natalia had felt a little left out of Emma and Caitlin's friendship, too.

"Yeah." Natalia's voice had been a little louder this time, and they both looked up at Mr. Thomas in case he noticed. But he had his back to them, writing information about the last field trip of the year on the whiteboard. "Yeah, I felt like . . . Emma's my cousin and you're my best friend, and you guys didn't even like each other back in September. I just felt like *I* used to be the connection between you and Emma, and now you have your own friendship. But then I realized that was a *good* thing. I'm glad we're all friends now."

Caitlin reached over and gave Natalia's arm a brief squeeze. "I am, too. But you're my *best* friend. Definitely. Always."

The intercom crackled, and Caitlin looked up, expecting to hear some kind of school-wide announcement. Instead, the school secretary's voice came through. "Mr. Thomas, would you please send Caitlin Moore,

Natalia Martinez, Zoe Martinez, and Emma Blake to the office?"

A chorus of "Ooh, you're in trouble" rose up from some of the more immature boys in the class. Caitlin's stomach swooped.

"Okay," Mr. Thomas called back, and then said, "You can take your bags, girls, and go straight to your next class when you're done in the office. Homeroom's almost over."

Glancing nervously at each other, Caitlin and the others gathered up their stuff and filed out into the hall. Once they were out there with the door closed behind them, Emma voiced all their fears. "Are we in trouble?" No one answered.

On the walk to the office, Caitlin felt sick. Anxious thoughts kept churning through her mind: Had Mr. Patel changed his mind and decided they needed to be punished for cheating? She didn't even know what the school punishment for cheating was. Detention? *Suspension?* Her parents would be furious if she got suspended. She couldn't even imagine what they'd do.

Or maybe, when Mr. Patel had called the contest organizers to report what had happened, *they* had decided there had to be some kind of punishment. Could they make the school pay a fine? And what would the school do to Caitlin and the others then?

She looked at the others as they headed toward the office doors. To her ears, their footsteps sounded disturbingly loud in the quiet of the between-classes hall. Emma was pale, and Zoe and Natalia were walking close together, their arms brushing. She could tell they were all thinking along the same lines as she was.

When they walked into the office, Mr. Patel was standing behind the reception desk, chatting with the secretary. "Oh, good, here you are," he said, smiling at them.

He wouldn't smile if we were in trouble, would he? Caitlin thought, confused.

"Good news!" Mr. Patel announced. "We're back in the state finals for the trivia competition!"

Caitlin felt like the breath had been knocked out of her. "*What?*" she gasped. "Why?"

"I thought we weren't going to be allowed to compete," Zoe said, sounding a little indignant.

Mr. Patel was grinning widely now. "Apparently the committee thought about the situation and was concerned that, if you were accidentally sent the questions for the contest, there was a possibility that they might have also been sent to some of the other competitors. They couldn't be sure that anyone else who got it would be as honest as you four about coming forward."

"So, what did they decide?" Caitlin asked. "The contest is still happening. They're not going to just scrap all the questions, are they?"

Mr. Patel pointed at her. "Exactly! They're going to have to come up with a whole new, completely different set of questions. And so, there's no need for our team to forfeit the competition."

Caitlin felt her mouth drop open. *We're going to be in the competition after all?* She'd gotten so resigned to the idea that by admitting they'd looked at the questions, they'd given up their chance to compete. It had been awful, but she had understood why they'd had to drop out.

But . . . apparently not anymore.

Everything seemed slightly blurred and distant to her as they thanked Mr. Patel and, hanging on to each other, found themselves back out in the hallway. Caitlin was so shocked that it felt like she was in a dream.

Natalia grabbed Caitlin in a hug. "I can't believe it!" she gasped. Caitlin's vision cleared, and her heart started hammering hard. When Natalia let go of her, Zoe hugged her, and then Emma.

"Are you okay, Caitlin?" Emma asked, letting go of her with a frown. Caitlin realized she hadn't said anything, and now all three of her friends were looking at her with concern.

She made a conscious effort to pull herself together. "Do you know what this means?" she demanded.

Natalia and Zoe exchanged puzzled looks. "Um, that we're back in the competition?" Zoe asked.

"Yes," Caitlin said. "And the competition is in two days, and the last couple times we studied, we spent all our time on the only questions we know for sure *won't* be on the test. We need to get to work!"

Chapter Eleven

The state championship was being held in Baltimore this year, more than an hour-and-a-half drive away from Waverly, and was at a much bigger and fancier hall than the previous competitions had been.

"Wow," Caitlin said, gazing around as they entered the auditorium. It seemed huge, with rows and rows of padded red velvet seats, many of which were already filled. A glittering chandelier hung from the ceiling high above. The stage looked vast and had long red curtains looped back at the sides. Caitlin didn't think of herself as shy—not like Emma—but she felt a little nervous looking up at that big stage.

Even though there were only six teams competing— the three semifinalist teams from Eastern Maryland

and the three from Western Maryland—the audience was much larger than at the previous competitions.

Natalia gasped and gripped Caitlin's arm hard. "Oh, my gosh. Do you see *that*? There are TV cameras here!" At the back of the room, several adults fiddled with camera equipment marked with the logo of a local station. Natalia craned her neck to see, bouncing with excitement.

Emma looked terrified. "We're not going to be on *television*, are we?"

"I'm sure they're just going to put a little, *tiny* bit about the contest on the local news. We probably won't be on it," Caitlin said soothingly.

"I would *love* to be on TV," Natalia breathed. "Do you think they'd interview me if I went over there?"

"Get your head in the game," Caitlin said firmly. "There will be plenty of time to try to become a TV star once we've won."

Natalia rolled her eyes. "Yes, ma'am."

Caitlin spotted Mr. Patel waving to them from the front of the auditorium, where the front rows were reserved for the trivia teams. "Look, he's saved us some seats."

When they reached him, Mr. Patel handed Caitlin the schedule for the first round. "You're up against Lakeside Middle School in the first round," he told them. "The team is all eighth graders. You'll be the second matchup."

We've beaten older kids before, Caitlin reassured herself, wishing that they weren't all eighth graders.

As the girls took their seats, Caitlin turned and waved at her parents. They'd dressed up for this, her dad in a sports jacket and her mom in a pretty blue dress. She smoothed her own dress—yellow with white flowers— and thought how nice they all looked, and how dressing up made the competition feel like even more of an event. Robbie shot her a wink and a thumbs-up.

As the audience settled, the moderator walked out on stage. "Welcome!" she said. "We're proud of our scholars, who have studied so hard and learned so much on their way here." She went on, praising the competitors— "each of whom is already a champion"—and explaining the rules of the contest. "And now, our first competitors!

Please welcome the teams from the Baltimore Latin School and Towson Middle School." The moderator led the applause as two teams of kids walked out onto the stage and took their seats at the tables.

Caitlin watched attentively. Towson was strong on nature and on history, but weak on literature. The Baltimore Latin School was doing well in history, literature, and sports, but wasn't that great on nature, especially facts about animals. Both teams seemed like they were okay on art, but not as good as Zoe: Towson fell behind on a question about cubism, which even Caitlin knew had something to do with Picasso.

In the end, Baltimore Latin won and took a spot in the final round. The moderator came out and spoke again, but now Caitlin was barely listening. *We're up next!* She turned and looked at her team. Emma was listening attentively to the moderator, so pale that Caitlin could see faint golden freckles on her cheeks. Natalia was scanning the other competitors. And Zoe was busily doodling in her sketchbook.

"Guys!" Caitlin whispered. "It's our turn!" Emma

nodded, her eyes wide, but Natalia looked startled and Zoe jumped and nearly dropped her sketchbook.

Just then, the moderator announced, "Please welcome Lakeview Middle School and Waverly Middle School." Caitlin and her teammates got hurriedly to their feet and filed up onto the stage behind the Lakeview team, which was all big, older-looking boys.

Caitlin took a deep breath. *It's fine. We can handle them.* Beside her, Emma, who had been so tense and miserable while they were waiting to compete, now looked cool and completely unruffled. They exchanged small smiles, and then Caitlin poised her hand above the buzzer.

"First question," the moderator said. "How long can a Nile crocodile remain underwater without surfacing for air?"

Bzzz! Caitlin hit the buzzer first, but she had no idea. She looked to Natalia.

"Crocodiles are so cool," Natalia whispered. "Two hours!"

"Two hours," Caitlin said.

"Correct."

"What is the only state that touches just one other state?"

The Lakeview captain beat her to the buzzer that time. "Maine," he said confidently, and the moderator nodded.

"Correct!"

Bzzz!

"Georgia O'Keeffe was known for her close-up pictures of flowers."

Bzzz!

"The Civil War was fought from 1861 to 1865."

Bzzz!

"The Los Angeles Dodgers used to be known as the Brooklyn Dodgers."

The score ping-ponged back and forth. (They even answered a question on Ping-Pong, thanks to Emma's research on sports and games. She knew that it originated in Victorian England.) First, Waverly pulled ahead, and then Lakeview, each missing a point here or there but steadily building up their scores. The captain of the Lakeview team glared at Caitlin fiercely whenever she beat him to the buzzer, but she stuck her chin stubbornly in the air and refused to be intimidated. It was his own fault if he couldn't keep up with them.

They were one point ahead when they came to the last question. Caitlin leaned forward, her hand above the buzzer.

"What were the pen names the Brontë sisters were originally published under?"

I know this. Caitlin slammed her hand down, but she was a fraction of a second too late.

Oh no. The Lakeview team was going to catch up.

But the captain and his team had their heads together and were still talking to each other, urgently and quietly. Caitlin sat up straighter to watch them. Did they not know? They had gotten to the buzzer first, but if they didn't know the answer, they were going to lose.

The captain of the Lakeview team leaned forward, looking doubtful. "Victoria and . . . Alice, uh, Evans?" he guessed.

"I'm sorry, Lakeview, that's incorrect," the moderator told them. "Waverly, do you have an answer?"

Joy shot through Caitlin. She was sure of this one. "Currer, Ellis, and Acton Bell," she said triumphantly.

It was easy to remember because they'd used the same initials as their real names: Charlotte, Emily, and Anne Brontë.

Caitlin shook hands with the Lakeview team captain, excitement bubbling up inside her. They were through to the final three. Just one more round, and they might be headed to New York.

They went back to their seats, and Caitlin prepared to scope out the last teams in the first round: Sacred Heart School—the ones whose classmates had all come to watch—and a very serious-looking team from a school called Valley Park Middle School.

Emma watched, too, way calmer now that she'd fought off her stage fright and they'd made it through the first round. Zoe went back to drawing, ignoring the competition going on in front of them.

Valley Park's team seemed serious and methodical. After watching for a few minutes, Caitlin noticed that their captain turned to one teammate for history questions, another for science, a third for sports. *They're doing the same thing we did*, she decided. *Everybody has their specialty subject area.*

Next to her, Natalia shifted around, turning back and forth to look at the audience. "I think I know that girl from camp," she whispered at last.

Caitlin glanced briefly back over her shoulder, too. "What girl?"

"That girl from Towson Middle School, with the curly hair." Natalia pointed at her. "I'm going to go talk to her."

"Okay, but be back before the second round," Caitlin whispered back. It was like Natalia to reach out and try to talk to people at a competition like this—whether the girl turned out to be who Natalia thought she was or not, Caitlin guessed that she and Natalia would be friends by the end of the day. Caitlin smiled. It made her feel good that someone who made friends as easily as Natalia did had chosen Caitlin as her *best* friend.

Sacred Heart's team was good, and they had a big cheering section in the audience, but Valley Park was better. Slowly but surely, they widened the gap between their scores.

"Congratulations, Valley Park Middle School!" the moderator said at last. As the team captains shook hands, she added, "We're going to take a fifteen-minute break before moving on to the final round to select our new state champions!"

Good, Caitlin thought. Most of the people in the auditorium were filing out to stretch their legs or use the bathroom, but she and her teammates could use this time to prepare for the last round. She turned around and scanned the auditorium until she spotted Natalia near the back, talking eagerly to the curly-haired girl and one of her teammates. Caitlin waved to her to join them.

"Hey!" Natalia said, bouncing into her seat a few moments later. "She wasn't who I thought she was after all, but she was super-nice. She was telling me all about horseback riding, and now I think we need to add that to our summer plan for becoming extraordinary. Extraordinary horseback riding."

"Sounds fun," said Caitlin. "Does *extraordinary* horseback riding involve some kind of tricks?" Without waiting for an answer, she dug into her bag and pulled out four small bottles of water. "Here." She handed them around to the others. "Hydrate. It's very important to keep your brain working at peak capacity."

"Are you sure 'capacity' is the word you want?" Emma asked doubtfully. She unscrewed her water bottle and took a sip.

"Peak ability. Whatever." Caitlin wasn't going to be distracted. "I've been watching our competition and they're really good."

"They definitely are," Emma agreed.

"But so are we," Caitlin went on. "It's just going to come down to luck, and what questions the moderator asks. Let's spend this whole break reviewing. If we lose, I want it to be because we had bad luck and got questions we didn't know, not because we forgot something we *did* know."

"Absolutely, Trivia Queen," Zoe said, an affectionate note in her voice. "I knew you were going to say we should spend the break studying. Want to see my drawing of us first?"

"Um." It was important to make every study moment count. But Caitlin actually *did* want to see how Zoe had drawn them. "Okay."

Zoe passed her the notebook she'd been doodling on.

The drawings of them were very recognizable, sitting

behind a long table, a buzzer in front of cartoon Caitlin, obviously all ready to compete. Zoe herself was smirking knowingly up at the viewer, while Emma, visibly tense but with a tiny smile, had a speech balloon that said, in shaky letters, *Actually, I'm feeling much better.* Cartoon Natalia's hair flew in every direction, and she was grinning like a maniac. And cartoon Caitlin had a stack of index cards clutched in her hands and was saying, with an intense stare, *The most important thing is to learn EVERYTHING.*

Caitlin giggled. "There are worse mottos," she said. The drawings were funny, and somehow they looked just like them.

At her insistence, they all rehydrated with the bottled water and spent the few minutes they had left of break reviewing.

"The order of taxonomy, how scientists classify animals," she said to Natalia. "Can you name them?" Natalia hesitated and Caitlin added, "King Phillip . . ."

Brightening, Natalia said, "Oh, yeah, that's a good one. King Phillip Came Over From Great Spain. Kingdom, phylum, class, order, family, genus, species."

Caitlin burst into applause. "I'm so proud of you," she said, sort of joking and not joking at all. Natalia had studied hard.

~

The break went by fast. Long before Caitlin felt like they had reviewed anywhere near enough, they were called back onto the stage, where a third table had been added.

"The final round is a little different, because, as you can see, three teams compete for the state championship," the moderator told the audience. She explained how the state semifinals had worked and how each semifinal competition had sent three competitors to the finals: three from Eastern Maryland and three from Western Maryland. "And those six have now been narrowed down to the top three middle school trivia teams in the state," she said. "The winner will become our state champion and go on to compete for the national title."

The audience clapped and cheered, and then the competition began.

It was weird competing with two other teams instead

of one. Caitlin felt like her rhythm was off. She couldn't keep an eye on both other team captains at the same time, and she couldn't predict when they were reaching for the buzzer.

Still, her own team was doing fine, she told herself.

Bzzz!

"Polar bears only hibernate if they're pregnant."

Bzzz!

"Rudyard Kipling wrote a book about a mongoose called *Rikki-Tikki-Tavi*."

She felt like her whole world was focused on the buzzer in front of her, and like her energy was powered by her teammates, each of them as laser-focused as she was.

And then she took a deep breath and realized that they were at a crucial moment. Baltimore Latin School had pulled ahead: They had seven points, out of twenty questions in the round. Caitlin and her team had six. Valley Park Middle School *also* had six points.

If Baltimore Latin answered the next question correctly, they would win. If either Caitlin's team or Valley

Park got the answer, that team would move on to a sudden death round with Baltimore Latin, and the third team would be eliminated.

"This is it," she murmured, and Emma nudged her supportively.

"Hit that buzzer," she whispered. "You can do it."

"Who was the only US president to get married in the White House while in office?"

Caitlin moved fast, hitting the buzzer so hard it moved across the table.

"Waverly Middle School," the moderator said.

Married in the White House. Caitlin's stomach felt weird and heavy. She had *no* idea. She turned hopefully to the others. Natalia was twisting her hair. Zoe was frowning. Emma shook her head. "None of us know," she whispered. "It couldn't be George Washington, because he never lived in the White House, but it could be anyone else."

"I don't think it was anybody after World War II," Zoe whispered, "because I feel like we would have seen pictures of that in history books and stuff."

"Waverly, you have ten seconds," the moderator said.

"Just go for it," Natalia whispered. "Say anything."

Caitlin's head was spinning. She couldn't think of many first ladies from before the late-twentieth century. There was Eleanor Roosevelt, who had been a big supporter of human rights. "Franklin D. Roosevelt," she blurted at the last moment.

"I'm sorry, that's incorrect," the moderator said.

The Baltimore Latin captain hit his buzzer.

"The Baltimore Latin School."

He turned and talked to his teammates. *Please don't know the answer,* Caitlin thought. She didn't want to lose.

Turning back to the moderator, the Baltimore Latin captain said, "Grover Cleveland."

"Correct!" said the moderator. "Congratulations, Baltimore Latin School. You are the new Maryland State Trivia Champions!"

And that was it. A pang of disappointment shot through Caitlin. She blinked back tears, stuck her chin out, and went to shake hands with the other captains.

She even managed to say "Congratulations" to the Baltimore Latin captain and to sound like she meant it.

Then she returned to her teammates. They were hanging back at the edge of the stage. Like her, they didn't seem quite ready to go meet their families. "I'm sorry, you guys," she said. "I really wanted us to win."

Zoe frowned. "What are you apologizing for?"

"Well, I gave the wrong answer," Caitlin said. "I shouldn't have guessed Franklin Roosevelt. I bet they were married way before he became president."

"It was a good guess," Emma said. "And you've been a really good captain, Caitlin. I know we argued, but you kept us on track, and we all learned a lot."

"Yeah?" Caitlin said. She looked down at her feet, feeling herself smile a little bit. "We didn't do so badly, did we? We're one of the top three trivia teams in the state. We're the champions of our county."

"Yeah, we definitely know more trivia than anyone else in school," Natalia said. "I'll be amazing people with my random animal facts for years. Did you know that giant Arctic jellyfish have tentacles that are over a hundred feet long? Just imagine that."

"Ick," said Emma. "I'm glad I don't swim in the Arctic Ocean."

"I guess we did do pretty well," Caitlin agreed. "We should be proud. I *am* proud, of all of us. And we can do even better next year."

Her friends exchanged glances. Natalia flung an arm around Caitlin's shoulders. "I bet we can, but we're not even going to *think* about it until September. This summer, I have other plans for becoming extraordinary. Just because we didn't win the trivia contest doesn't mean we can't find cool things to do."

"I'd like to learn to scuba dive," Emma said.

"I bet my mom would let us paint a big mural on the walls of my and Natalia's bedroom," Zoe suggested. "I'm picturing a woodland scene." She spread out her arms wide. "Like, huge trees. Redwoods. All across our walls."

"We could become great cooks," Natalia offered. "I'd like to learn to bake bread, at least."

Caitlin pulled her friends into a group hug. They

hadn't won the contest, but she was happy anyway. Who cared if they got to go to New York City this year? There was always next year's trivia competition—they would be even better prepared and win that one for sure.

"It's going to be a great summer, I can see that already," Caitlin told her friends. "And whatever we do, let's do it together."

Read Emma's story!

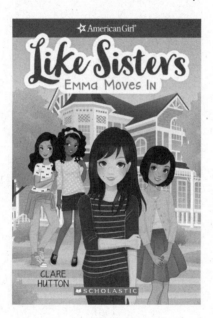

Chapter One

Things We Absolutely HAVE To Do:

1. Have a cookout

Well, that will be easy, Emma thought, wiggling her feet under the airline seat in front of her. By the time she and her parents finally got to Waverly, Uncle Luis would be flipping burgers on the grill while her mom's twin sister, Aunt Alison, and all the cousins arranged salads and desserts on the big outdoor trestle table.

Last year, her family had gotten there the evening before the annual family barbecue, and Emma and her two favorite cousins, twins Natalia and Zoe, had made up their own brownie recipe. They mixed in not just walnuts and chocolate chips, but dried pineapple, coconut, raisins, peanuts, and marshmallows. It had been Natalia's idea—Zoe had been skeptical, and Emma had thought maybe they should play it safe and follow the real recipe—but Natalia had insisted, and she'd been right. The brownies had been delicious. Emma's mouth watered at the memory.

2. Swim

Back home in Seattle, the water was too cold to swim in the ocean. Emma swam in indoor swimming pools, competing in relays and races. It was fun, and she was good at it. She liked the smell of chlorine and the stretch of her muscles. Swimming in the warm, sun-splashed water of the Chesapeake Bay with Natalia and Zoe was even better, though.

3. Sparklers

At night after the barbecue, everyone—even the grown-ups—would light sparklers out in the front yard of Zoe and Natalia's house, writing their names in light. It was tradition, and their family cared about tradition.

4. Bonfire on the beach

Some evening this week, when the weather was just right, they would build a fire of driftwood on the beach and toast marshmallows to make s'mores. Natalia liked hers so dark they were almost black, and Zoe preferred hers untoasted, but Emma would turn hers patiently until they were a perfect, even golden brown all the way around.

5. Knitting with Grandma Stephenson

Over Christmas, Grandma had started all three of them making scarves. Emma had chosen blue and white; Zoe, black and purple; and Natalia, red and turquoise. Emma had tried to finish the scarf on her own after she and her parents had gone back home, but the yarn had gotten tangled and she'd dropped too many stitches. Finally, she'd given up in frustration. It was too hard, and not as much fun by herself.

A pang went through Emma's chest at the thought of her grandmother. Back in the spring, Grandma Stephenson had fallen on the stairs of Seaview House, her big, wonderful Victorian home, and broken her hip. She was okay—everyone said she was going to be just fine—but she had left Seaview House and moved in with Zoe and Natalia's family, where their other grandma, Uncle Luis's mom, Abuelita, already lived.

Emma's mom had told her the living situation was only temporary, but it had been going on for months now. What if Grandma wasn't really okay? No, her mom wouldn't have said Grandma was going to be fine unless it was true.

But the beautiful house where generations of Emma's family had lived was shuttered and silent. Emma's mom said that Seaview House would be too big for Grandma Stephenson to take care of by herself even when she was fully recovered.

At the thought of Seaview House empty, Emma felt her throat go tight, and she swallowed back the feeling before it turned into tears. It would be silly to cry over a *house* when the important thing was that Grandma was okay. Determined not to think about Seaview House, she turned back to her list.

Emma hesitated, her pencil resting on the paper, not sure about whether to leave knitting on the list. They could knit just as well in the living room of Natalia and Zoe's house as they had in the parlor at Seaview House, of course. But maybe Grandma didn't feel like doing projects anymore since she'd been hurt. Should she scratch that one out?

Even if Grandma hadn't changed, knitting wasn't really a summer thing, and Natalia and Zoe might have already finished their scarves with Grandma while Emma wasn't there. Emma pushed away the fleeting thought, *Not fair.* She knew she couldn't expect everyone in Waverly to just wait for her to come back before doing anything fun together.

Next to her, Emma's dad gave a little snore, and she glanced up as he slouched farther down against the airplane window, his glasses perched crookedly on his nose and his mouth open. Emma's mom looked up from her laptop screen at the same time and caught Emma's eye just as her dad snorted. They both giggled.

"He's been working hard on the new menu," her mom said. "This nap is just what he needs. He'll be ready to ride the waves with you girls by the time we get there."

Emma grinned. Her dad had the most ridiculous bathing suit—bright pink with wild purple and turquoise tropical flowers on it—but she liked how he came out into the water or onto the beach in his crazy bathing suit and played with them, instead of just hanging out with the other grown-ups. Last summer, he'd helped them and Zoe and Natalia's little brothers build a huge sand castle with a pebble-covered drawbridge and turrets reaching up to the sky.

She felt a sudden surge of affection for her parents. She liked their tight little unit of three: her mother, her father, and herself.

But sometimes she couldn't help envying Zoe and Natalia for having not just their parents and each other, but also their little brothers (even if Tomás and Mateo were bratty sometimes), and Grandma Stephenson, and Abuelita, and living near Uncle Dean and Aunt Bonnie, whose own kids were mostly away at college and brand-new jobs. They had tons of family, right in their town. Right in their *house*.

They—the whole of her mom's side of the family, except for Emma and her parents—all lived in Waverly, a small town on the Chesapeake Bay, where the family had lived for generations. Natalia and Zoe went to the school where Emma's mom and their mom (Aunt Alison) had gone, along with their brother (Uncle Dean). The school was right down the street from Seaview House, where her mom's grandparents, and more generations before that, had lived.

It must be nice to *belong* somewhere so much that everyone knew you and you knew every inch of the whole town. Emma lived in Seattle now, but two years ago they'd lived in San Francisco, before her mom got a job at a different law firm. Natalia and Zoe had lived in the same house their whole lives.

Emma's mom went back to her computer screen, squinting at a long, boring-looking work document. And Emma picked up her pencil and looked down at her list again.

6. Finish the Violet story

She and Natalia had started a story last summer—all about a girl named Violet who had a talking dog that only Violet could understand and the trouble he'd gotten her into. They had laughed a lot writing it, and Zoe had drawn really funny pictures of steam coming out of Violet's ears because she was so angry and of her innocent-faced dog looking as if he had no idea what had happened or *why* everything was such a mess.

Did Natalia still have the story? They hadn't had time to work on it over Christmas. A little ball of anxiety expanded in Emma's chest. There was never enough *time*. In just a week, she'd be on a plane heading back to Seattle again.

The pilot's voice came over the intercom, interrupting her thoughts. "We're now approaching our final descent into Baltimore. Please return your seatbacks to their upright position and secure tray tables to the seatback in front of you."

There was a ton more she'd meant to write, but she was out of time again. Quickly, Emma scribbled the most important thing.

7. Cousin pact

There were so many more things she could have listed, so many things she wanted to fit into the one week they'd have with the rest of the family. But they'd make time for the pact.

She latched the tray table and put her seat upright as her mom shut down her laptop. Next to her, her dad yawned himself awake.

"How're you doing, kiddo?" he asked. "Excited to get to the house and see everybody?"

"Yeah," said Emma. She folded her list and stuffed it into the pocket of her backpack. "I just wish we could stay longer this time." She saw her parents exchange a look and added, "I know we can't. It would be fun to be with Natalia and Zoe for longer, though."

She understood why they could only come to Waverly for a few days over Christmas and for a week in the summer. Her dad was the head chef at Harvest Moon, a restaurant specializing in comfort food in Seattle, and her mom was an environmental lawyer who worked to protect the wetlands. They didn't get much time off, and Waverly was far away from Seattle. Her parents had gone over it with her a million times when she was younger and didn't understand why she couldn't see her cousins more often.

"There's a lot of stuff I want to do when we're there," she tried to explain, "and I know I won't see Natalia and

Zoe again till Christmas. I try to cram everything in, but there's never quite enough time."

Emma's dad patted her back, and her mom reached out and tucked a strand of Emma's long hair behind her ear. "We never get quite enough time with the people we love," she said sympathetically, "but try not to worry about deadlines and fitting everything you want to do in. Just concentrate on spending time with your cousins and having fun."

Emma nodded, feeling anticipation begin to spread through her. She *would* have fun. The plane's wheels hit the runway with a bump, and she realized that the whole golden, glorious week with the family was spread out before her, about to begin.

American Girl®

A group of girls so close, they're just

Like Sisters

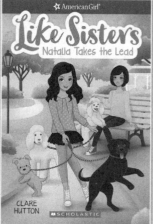

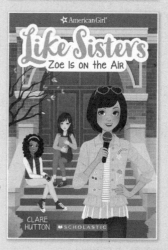

Join Jasmine, Sofia, Keiko, and Madison as they bond over their love of animals!

scholastic.com

AGFOREVERFRIEN